# 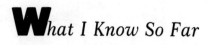What I Know So Far

*Also by Gordon Lish*

*Dear Mr. Capote*

# **W**hat<br>**W**I Know<br>**W**So Far

**G**ORDON<br>**L**ISH

A WILLIAM ABRAHAMS BOOK

*Holt,<br>Rinehart<br>and Winston<br>New York*

Published by Holt, Rinehart and Winston,
383 Madison Avenue, New York, New York 10017.
Published simultaneously in Canada
by Holt, Rinehart and Winston of Canada, Limited.
Library of Congress Cataloging in Publication Data
Lish, Gordon.
What I know so far.
"A William Abrahams book."
I. Title.
PS3562.I74W48   1983   813'.54   83-12980
ISBN 0-03-070609-2
First Edition
Printed in the United States of America
10 9 8 7 6 5 4 3 2 1

Grateful acknowledgment is made to the editors of the
publications in which these stories first appeared:
*Ploughshares, The Paris Review, Antioch Review,
Bennington Review, Plum, The New York Times,
Esquire, New England Review, Mississippi Review,
The Malahat Review, The Carleton Miscellany,
Crazyhorse, Columbia, The Missouri Review.*

"What Is Left To Link Us" has also
appeared in *Avenue* Magazine.

ISBN 0-03-070609-2

*To W.A. and C.O.*

*Of the world as it exists, it is impossible to be enough afraid.*

—T. W. ADORNO

# Contents

**O**ne

# **E**verything I Know

*The wife insisted she would tell her version* first. I was instantly interested because of the word.

The husband stood by in readiness. Or perhaps his version still needed work.

She took a breath, grinned, and got right to the most alarming part first. At least to what she wished us—and the husband?—to regard as the part that had most alarmed her.

She said she waked to find a man in her bed. Not the husband, of course. The husband, she said, was next door, visiting with a friend. She said the husband often did this, spent the evening hours visiting, next door or somewhere else. At any rate, the wife said she did not scream because fear had made her speechless. She said that speechlessness was a common enough reaction, and to this the husband nodded in enthusiasm.

But she was able to get to her feet and run. She ran out the front door. She said she ran three blocks to a telephone booth and called the police.

"My God," I said. "That's terrifying."

"I know," she said, and smiled.

I took her smile to be a common enough reaction.

I said, "And you were so terrified that you ran away from the house with the man and your little boy still in it?"

"Isn't it amazing?" the wife said. "That's how scared you can get."

"You don't need to tell me," I said. "But just think."

"Oh," she said, "they're not interested in kids."


The husband took a breath, and then started up his version, not one word about which part was the worst.

He said he came in by the back door, exercising great care to quiet the key because it was, after all, late. He said he did likewise with the action of his tread. But then he saw the front door wide open—and so he stepped quickly to the little boy's room, and saw that the little boy was safe in his bed.

"You see?" the wife said.

I said, "Thank God."

"I went to our bedroom next," the husband said.

He said he saw the bed empty and the bathroom door closed.

"Good God," I said, "the rapist is in there!"

My wife said, "For pity's sake, let *him* tell it."

The husband said he went weak with shock. He said he understood it was useless to stand there exhorting himself to open the bathroom door. He said he was simply certain of it—the wife would be in there, dead.

"Can you blame him?" the wife said.

The husband said, "So I sat down on the bed and called the police."

Then they both smiled.

"The rapist wasn't in there?" I said.

*"Please,"* my wife said.

The husband said he could barely talk. He said the police kept urging him to speak up.

"My wife's missing!"

This is what the husband said he screamed into the telephone, but that the police said no, not to worry, she's in a phone booth just blocks from the house.


"That's awful," my wife said.

I said, "But the bathroom."

The husband said, "I didn't touch that door until the police got there—and when they did, of course it was empty."

"Of course," I said. "Is there a window in there?"

The wife nodded.

"Open," the husband said, satisfied.

"That's the way he got out," the wife promptly added.

"The rapist," my wife said, just as quickly.


I've told you everything I know. I've told it to you precisely as it was revealed to me. But there is something in these events that I don't understand. I think there is something that those two people—no, three—aren't telling me. I sometimes think it must be staring me right in the face, just the way the three of them were when the story was all finished.

# **H**ow to **W**rite a Poem

*I tell you, I am no more a sucker for this* thing of poetry than the next fellow is. I mean, I can take it or leave it—a certain stewarded pressure, some modulated pissing and moaning, the practiced claims of a seasonal heart. But once in a blue moon I have in hand a poem whose small unfolding holds me to its period. It needn't be any great shakes, such a poem. I don't care two pins for what its quality is. Christ, no—literature's not what I look to poetry for.

Fear is.

You know. Fear—like *terror*.

You keep your head on straight, there'll be this breeze you'll start to feel, a sort of dainty susurration of the words. That's when you can bet the poor sap's seen it coming at him—an ordinary universe, the itemless clutter of an unraveling world. First chance he gets, it's a whole new ballgame, touching bases while he races home free, that little telltale wind on the page you're looking at as the gutless poet starts to work up speed.

Maybe I don't like poets—or people. But I just love to catch a poet at it, and then to test myself against the thinglessness that made him cut and run. What I do is I pick it up where the poet's nerve dumped him, where he just couldn't stand to see there's still nothing in a place where something never was.

It's no big deal. You just face down what he, in his chickenheart, couldn't. Then you type your version up and sign your name. Next thing you do is get it printed as your own, sit back and listen to them call you brave.

It's the safest theft, a stolen poem—and who, tell me, doesn't steal something? Besides, show me what a poet dares demand his right to. A public reading? Public subsidy? But certainly not a grand banality. Least of all the very one his cowardice dishonored! Forget it—this is a person who is afraid.


What brings me to these brusque disclosures is an experience of recent vintage, a poem I took over from a certain someone who is a woman, and have since passed off—not without applause—as my own.

Nothing to it.

Just you watch.

The text—I mean the one that came before me—tells us of a thing as follows: two women, the poet and a widow, the bereaved missus of the lover of the poet.

7

For how long had the lovers been lovers?
Long enough.
And the deceased deceased?
A less long time than that.
Whatever the precise numbers, we are talking about an adulterous liaison of the usual order.
Routine. The loved and the loveless.
Of course, the poet is herself married. But since her spouse never enters the poem by more than intimation, we are led, I think, to conclude that his relation to all this is of no concern and of less importance. I mean, insofar as people going and fucking whom they weren't supposed to, the poet's spouse doesn't figure into any of this at all. He does not *press*, that is—at least not on the mounting prospect of what we're sure must be coming.

Not so the dead man's wife. What I am suggesting is— what is suggested by the poet in the poem (oh yes, the poet, as I said, is *in* the poem, in the poem and speaking)—is that an air of discovery thickens over things very greatly: the unsuspecting widow, her husband's sneaky copulations. But, naturally, that's where we're headed, where the original text is taking us—toward exposure, toward widow-know-all.

(As for the one party the poem pays no mind to, now that the poet's version has been published—in not nearly so distinguished a setting as mine was—doesn't *he* know all too, even as I write this?

But perhaps the spouses of poets don't need poetry.

Perhaps that's why the poet was in this fix in the first place.

Fair enough—we'll stand agreed the poet had her reasons.)

What does it matter one way or the other, the poet's hubby, what he knows or what he doesn't? It's plain we're not required to render him more than passing notice. The poet urges as much.

One dismissive reference.


What happens is this.

In the poem, remember?

We see the poet and the widow at the widow's. Newly back from the cemetery? We're not informed. Just this—a blustery day, late autumn, late morning, the women in pullovers and cardigans, grays, tans, tweeds, second sweaters draped over shoulders, legs scissored back under buttocks.

A living room, a fire. Comfy. Cozy.

Are the principals seated on the floor?

I think so. I like to think so.

What we're told is the poet's here to lend a hand— help sort the dead man's papers, be good company, a goodly solace, a presence in a very empty house. So we see the women being women together, being friends together, fingering what the dead man said.

(Was he a poet, too? More than likely. Nowadays, there are many, many poets.)

We see them grieving lightly, smoothing skirts, reminiscing, sipping tea, making tidy. Well, we hear this, see that—I don't recollect if the poet really keeps her senses keyed to this or that event. So we see or hear their speeches when they reach into a carton to read aloud a bit of this, a bit of that.

You know. Order, memory, fellowship. A little weeping. Women's shoulders, women's sweaters.

Nice.

When—you guessed it—there's the wife with her hand at the bottom of a carton, and then her hand up and out, a neat packet in it, envelopes, a certain shape and paper, a

certain fragrance, the dead man's record of the poet's in-
discretion—letters that record a passion, letters that give
account.

My God!

Etc., etc., etc.

But let's not be children here. It's not as bad as all that.
After all, the man's dead and buried. Quite beyond scolding.
The widow's seen plenty. The poet is a poet. Life is . . . life.

Oh, well.

So there we are (at the poet's placing), watching women
being wiser—hearing women cry a little, hearing women
laugh a little, and then at last, seeing them, as veterans will,
embracing.

I'm not so sure who speaks first, nor what the poet
said was said—the poet's poem being somewhere in my
household, but I being too caught up in this to get up to go
and check. Let's just say the widow says, "All these years,
all these years. And who *was* he? He was who you talked
to in these letters."

And the poet?

Who remembers?

But I expect she says whatever's said to someone being
spacious just for your benefit. Perhaps this: "No, no, no—
it was you who had the best of him, the substance, the
husband, the man." Etc., etc.

The deceased, in pursuit of this assertion, is then cel-
ebrated, in four deft lines, for his performance in the four
arduous capacities of husband, citizen, father, provider.

Is there guile in this? Does the poet mean for us to
take a tiny signal?

Consider—four roles, four lines? Why such a sweet
symmetry? Is this art or artfulness? And consider even further: Is there really any difference?

What's crucial is who's kidding—the poet in the poem or the poet outside it?

Balance, I really hate balance. A proper disproportion, that's the zippy thing.


So there they are, poet and widow, usurper and usurped. Unclothed as it were—even pretty close to naked—each of them jumpy to reach out and grab the nearest covering.

So they hurry up and bury their embarrassment in the terry-cloth offered up by bodies.

Another embrace. Sort of sisterly. Good hugging. But it goes from there to a thing you'd call carnal. At which point, the poem has furnished us with the bulk of its text, the day (get this!) having, in its pliant time, accomplished (the poet tells us) a like progress.

So it's dusk when the two women make their way to bed, to do what the poet then gives us to imagine. But before we know it, the poet reappears, having projected (she explains) her astral body back to the room where she'd left us. We see, via her sight, the letters lying strewn among the papers. We see teacups, saucers, purses, shoes, two outer sweaters. We see these things as things at first, items on the widow's Chinese carpet.

The rest of the poem?

Now there you have it! For it now labors to extract from the figure of these particulars a facsimile of the human spectacle, something serviceable in the way of meaning, the event quantified, the lesson learned.


This was the poem the poet published and that I—genius that I am for spotting where a work has turned away from the fearful vision in it—have since rewritten and passed along for eight dollars and the fun.

Now let me tell you what I did.

In my poem, nothing's different. Word for word, it's all the same—up until the astral body comes back for a summary. Just like the phony poet, I take a look around. I see the same artifacts, all the stuff that produced this emptiest of rooms.

I mean, I see the letters and the teacups and the sweaters and the shoes. These things and all the poet saw. But in my poem, where they are is on a span of decent-grade, wall-to-wall broadloom bought when the price was right.

Now you know what art is.

And notice, was I ever even once a person in that house?

Skip it. It's all the same to me—the goddamn fancy carpet, what's on it and its fucking whereabouts.

# **W**hat Is Left to Link Us

*I* *want to tell you about the undoing of a* man. He's not a fellow I ever knew very well. It is only the key erosions that built to his collapse that I know well enough, the handful of episodes that toppled this fellow from the little height he thought he had. I, in fact, was present at what you might call the critical moment. I mean the turning when our man was tipped, as it were, all the way over. As for the aftermath, how he has since fared in the grip of his ruin, that is a matter I know, and care, next to nothing about.

He had a marriage, children, and a second woman

whom he would see from time to time. As far as I could tell, his relations in all these respects were perfectly routine, the usual make-do life of a fellow residing in urban circumstance, a fellow in his forties, a moderately accomplished chap, which statement is meant to convey the impression of a fellow exceptionally able—if you will allow the assertion that passing accomplishment in our parlous times often calls for surpassing ability. His was that sort of urban circumstance—the work he did and where he did it. But that is just a particle of what I mean.

I won't trouble the initial sentences of this account with a description of the wife—for she will make her appearance later, when the critical moment arrives, and that will do nicely enough for her, given all that she really matters to what is unfolding. Nor is it central that you know much about the second woman—and indeed I do not have that much to tell you, considering that I laid eyes on the creature only once—just as I only once saw the woman that is the wife. It was at what I keep calling the critical moment that both women were first revealed to me, a coincidence you must have guessed would come.

As for the children, they are positively of no consequence at all.

What I did know, and knew well before the worst happened, was this: The man who is the subject of this little history had elected to end his relation with the second woman and had gone ahead and done something about it. At least that is what he said he had done when he later sought my attention over cocktails.

"To which she said what?" I said, trying to concentrate on particularities that interested me no more than the larger chronicle did.

But the fellow was waiting for this. He played with his glass and let a long silence draw the curtains aside. Then, suffering the phrases of his speech as if to place before me a parallel of the agony he chose to believe the second woman had struggled to surmount, our man said:

"'If that is what you want. If that is what you must have. All right.'"

"Splendid!" I said, and then I said, "You're well out of it, lad!" adding this latter more for reasons of ceremony and rhythm than in response to sound observation. Surely, I had nothing substantive to go on, no basis to judge the health of the fellow's spirit one way or the other, with or without his having the second woman to visit from time to time.

But it proved he was waiting for this also.

"I don't know," he said, pretending thought, it seemed to me.

"Of course you do!" I said. "Well out of it, I say!"

"I'd like to think so," he said, fingering his glass again, not drinking except in showily halting motions to his mouth. "But I don't know."

"Ah, well," I said, already fashioning up the sentence that would promote my exit.

You see, like the fellow whose collapse I record, I too reside in urban circumstance. I had planned to do the household grocery shopping after hours that Friday night—to do as I have always done in order that I not have to do the household grocery shopping the Saturday morning following, the number of shoppers being half as many Friday nights.

It was, and is, my custom—and I have come to be convinced that it is only the unbending observance of custom that sustains life in an urban circumstance. Those city persons strict and exact in their habits, and in possession of a broad array of them, survive. I believe I have seen examples persuasive enough on either side of the question to propose the rule.

The rule guides my conduct, in any case—whatever the validity of its content—and I had been too long drinking with this man and had good reason to be on my way.

Moreover, there was nothing I wanted to hear from him. There would be no surprises in anything he would say—because he knew exactly what to say.

In this he is identical to us all.

It is why I am not very interested in people—nor in myself. We all of us know exactly what to say, and say it—the man who sat with me making a drama out of his half-finished glass; I, speaking to him then and speaking to you now; you, reading and making your mind up about this page.

There is no escape from this. Nor is it any longer necessary to act as if there might be.

It was only necessary to say: "Look, my friend, there will be another one after this one. Better to have made an end to the thing and to get a new thing started."

He raised his eyes from his fraudulent musing, suddenly noticing me for the first time, I could tell.

"That's a shockingly childish and destructive suggestion," he said.

"You think so?" I said. "Perhaps my mind was elsewhere. What did I say?" I said.

He studied my expression for a time. I could see what he was after. But I would not let him have it.

"I'll get the check," he said, glancing at his wristwatch, and then, in a stylishly sweeping motion, lifting the same hand to signal for the waiter. "Got to run," he said, polishing off his drink and finishing with me as well. "Dinner's early and I haven't done the groceries yet."


During the course of the events I describe, my son's sled was stolen. Actually, it was removed from the premises by the custodian who services the little apartment building we live in. It was our custom to keep the sled right outside the door, propped against the hallway wall and ready for action—whereas it was the custodian's custom to complain that such storage of the sled interfered with his access to the carpet when he came once a week to clean it.

He comes Saturdays.

I could hear him out there with his industrial-caliber vacuum cleaner some Saturdays ago. The rumpus the thing creates is unmistakable, and I remember having to raise my voice to repeat "Your move." It was midday, a very lovely day, but we were home playing checkers, my boy and I, while his chicken pox healed and his mother was out running errands. It was only when she returned that the theft was discovered, the place where the Flexible Flyer had stood leaning now a small vacant patch of very clean carpet.

She called the landlord and she called the police.

The sled is, after all, irreplaceable, one of the last Flexible Flyers made of wood, a practice some while ago discontinued. We had to search the city to find it and buy it—and it was very satisfying to display it when the snow came and all those less exacting parents showed up with their deprived children and plastic.

I know he took it. I did not see him do it—but I know, I know.

It was a test of something, a clash of habits, custom pitted against custom—our will to show off our quality, his will to perform unstipulated work.

On the other hand, it is our carpet that is now uniformly clean those last few inches all the way to the wall. Not his!

I am not unwilling to be pleased by this.


At any rate, the man I am made to call my friend—because it is clumsy to keep referring to him otherwise, and I suppose

I must say I know him as well as I know anybody—telephoned me at my office the Monday following. Have I told you that we are in the same line of work?

The fellow often calls me at my office, to speak of business. It is the basis of our knowing one another—business, business things.

"Why did you say that?" my friend said.

"Say what?" I said.

"You know," he said. "Suggesting that I get another setup."

"Haven't you always? I thought that was your practice," I said.

"That's not the point," my friend said.

"Then what *is* the point?" I said.

"Skip it," my friend said, and hung up.

I was not the least bothered by any of this. To begin with, the man bored me—and conducted a private life no more interesting than mine. It is not that I am dismayed to hear a man's secrets; it is only that no one has any new ones. Besides, insofar as our joint concerns of a business nature go, the man's need of me was greater than my need of him. I think that is a fair enough statement. At all events, there is no question of it now. You must remember, the fellow has since been undone. When it comes to need now, he's the one who has it all.


It was at the toy store everyone around here uses that I saw the fellow next. There was nothing notable in our meeting there. We both have children; it is the best-stocked store midtown. One is always meeting someone one knows there.

"I'm worried," my friend said. "Please give me your attention."

"You have it," I said, and stared impressively at the two children whose hands he held.

"That's all right," he said.

"Yes," I said, "but it is not all right with me," at this using my eyes to usher his down to where they would notice the boy whose hand I held.

"Oh," my friend said. "Well, I'll call you."

He called that Monday.

"What's wrong with your kid?" he said.

"I thought you had something to tell me," I said.

"I do," he said, "but I never saw your kid before, and I was just thinking maybe my friend's got his sorrows too."

"Just chicken pox," I said, with my free hand squaring the papers on my desk.

"Takes a while for the scabs to heal, you know. Been through the shit twice with my two, and it can be a bitch, all right."

"Yes," I said.

"You're listening?" he said.

"Absolutely," I said, settling back now for whatever would come.

"I told you I was worried," he said. "Now here's why I'm worried."

I would not give him what he wanted. "Because you broke it off with her," I said. "And now you're worried that perhaps she's angry—and if she is angry, then maybe she will do something, make trouble—correct?"

"That's it," he said. "That's it exactly. So what do I do?"

"Do something to make her happy," I said. "Then she won't be angry."

"But what?" he said. "What could make her happy when she's angry?"

"Something special," I said. "Something uncommonly giving. Something truly extraordinary and charitable is what I usually recommend."

"You're right," he said, said he hoped my boy's face

would soon be without blemish, thanked me for my advice, and hung up.


The landlord claimed he was blameless, that he was not responsible for the loss of possessions I chose to store outside my door, that if I dared deduct the cost of the sled from my next check in payment of the rent, eviction would ensue. I remarked that the custodian was in the landlord's employ and that logic insisted the employer be held liable for thefts perpetrated by someone acting in performance of his employer's requirements. The landlord said that logic insisted nothing of the kind, that it was not his habit to retain the services of thieves, that his employee was not a thief, and that, moreover, I had no proof of theft.

The police said their hands were tied and that the loss, after all, was just a sled. But don't think I did not take down the oaf's badge number, the one who said just a sled.

As for the custodian, he has taken to coming on a weekday.

I am not at home weekdays.

My wife is. And she is afraid.


My friend called. I was about to leave, and perhaps I was not paying very close attention. Perhaps I should have examined his proposal more carefully. But it was a Wednesday, and Wednesdays I always vacate my office fifteen minutes sooner than is otherwise my habit, this to provide time to pick up the laundry before presenting myself at home.

I was courteous enough, I think. I do not think I was especially abrupt. But I expect I was not listening very closely. As a result, I not only failed to hear him well enough to counsel him with prudence, but of course I can also have no confidence that I will reproduce his sentences accurately. I believe, however, he said something approximate to this:

"I have the perfect plan. Just the thing. A really incredibly perfect idea, something extraordinary and giving, just as you said. You see, the thing was she was always complaining that I was unreasonably hesitant to let her share in my world, to be with the people I was with, and that sort of thing. You know the sort of thing I'm talking about—they do it all the time. I mean, once you're really involved with them, what they invariably want is to get really involved with you—hear about your friends, hear about your job, hear about your wife, all the dreariness that *you* of course *don't*. It gets that way with them, this pushing at you and pushing at you for more and more of your life. Oh, God, you must have had your own experiences with what I'm talking about. Honestly, I really don't think they can help themselves. I mean, they *know* better, don't they? I mean, they've got to know that if they keep it up they're going to end up pushing you too far. But they do it and they do it—and you go and do precisely what they don't want, hold back, hold more and more back, until it's yourself you figure you won't hand over anymore. The point is, that's exactly why my idea is right on the money. Because the idea I had is to give a party, a sort of going-away party— something that'll give her what she wants but end it at the same time. Just me and her and my two closest friends— you and this other friend I have—because I was always telling her about the two of you guys and she was always so terribly interested. It drove me nuts the way she was always asking to meet you two, me always having to invent excuses why she couldn't, these two great guys I know who happen to be my two best friends, you and this other guy."

I think I remember saying, "Please, be sensible, you and I are not precisely best friends." Or I may have said,

"Please, be sensible, that is a vulgar and lunatic idea."

I do not know what I said. I know that that night, when I had emptied out my briefcase to sort my papers, I found a notation giving this man's name, a restaurant, a date, a time. I still had this in my hand, amazed, when I went to ball up the laundry wrappings to stuff them in the trash. I don't know why I did not discard the slip of paper along with the rest. You will understand that it was not because I must have said yes to the fellow and was unwilling to go back on my word. Perhaps it was because I *had* said yes and was unwilling to dishonor the queer impetus that had made me do it. In any event, I put the reminder in my pocket and the laundry wrappings in the trash basket, lifted out the plastic liner, cinched it, and tossed the whole arrangement down the stairwell for the custodian to find it when he would.

The bastard.


There is chicken pox and there is chicken pox—and my boy had the second kind. We cautioned him not to scratch. Please understand that he is the sort of boy who respects a caution. I know he tried his best to resist. But a mad itching is a vile thing, and when it is rampantly out of control, there is nothing left for it but to claw.

He did his best.

I tell my wife the two lesions that left scars on his cheek will prove a trifling matter in the long term.

But she cries. She cries at night—when she thinks I am asleep and cannot hear.

Of course, it occurs to me to wonder if that is why she cries. It could be the loss of the sled that makes her cry. Or the specter of the cruel custodian. What kind of creature would take away what belongs to a child?

Or it could be something else she cries about.

I imagine he had grown anxious, after all—because I arrived second, and he said he had been sitting and waiting for almost an hour. Yet I was punctual, as is my custom. It was more than clear that he had been drinking for however long he had in fact waited. One would guess that he had come to regret what he had impulsively contrived, and it is to this that I assign his hasty and hearty indulgence.

"Are you afraid?" I said.

He tried to smile generously, but what his ambition produced was instead a lopsided impression of grossly disordered zeal. "What kind of thing is that to say?" he said, and threw his face toward the glass of whiskey that he had been elevating a degree or so off-plumb with his lips.

"Lad, you will never make it through the evening," I said.

"Will too," he said, not in the least equipped to rearrange the distortion that had seized his features. "Never felt more alive. Never more magnificently aware. You won't be sorry, buddy boy, I promise you."

I was going to ask my friend to give me a bit of information about the second man who was expected. Not that I really cared, but only to make conversation until the other diners arrived and the show got productively under way. It was then, while I was preparing to offer my inquiries and while my friend was laboring to raise his hand to call for a round, that I was strangely overcome by the oddest realization.

*I had never seen the custodian.*

The man might actually be anyone. The man could come running right up at me from anywhere—and I would never know that he was the man I should be ready for.

Had my wife seen the fellow?

Of course she must have—for had she not heard his complaint about the sled?

I know it will appear preposterous when I tell you that

the matter of the custodian, my disquiet over my never having seen him, so captured my attention that I've only the scantiest recollection of the drinking and the eating and the conversation that followed. I know that the second man proved a rather amiable chap and that we more or less discovered mutual interests. The woman was quite pleasant, really—handsome enough and not unintelligent. I cannot, I'm afraid I must say, recall much that anyone said, although I believe that the chitchat went agreeably forward and that the woman seemed genuinely pleased to be meeting the other fellow and me. Yet she made no great effort, as I remember, to draw either of us out—nor did she appear particularly interested in conversing with my friend. To sum it up, she was acceptably polite and sociable, if a stroke remote, and I for one intended to respect whatever distance she seemed to wish established.

I believe I kept to that mark.

I cannot say she showed the least surprise that our host was becoming progressively intoxicated by tumultuous leaps. I certainly was not—and, speaking for the other fellow, I am sure he wasn't, either. All in all, the evening was going off not a little gracefully, considering the potentially treacherous ground we occupied—it all resolving itself in a great deal of food and drink, a few peppery but convivial exchanges, and even a bit of downright comradely laughter.

I do remember that the food was unusually fine—in fact, I would say that the food was distinguished.

All this time, as I have told you, it was the custodian that remained chiefly in my consideration. Or, to put the point more descriptively, it was in my mind to get him out of it—and to focus my alertness on what was enacting itself before me. But I cannot say to what extent I was able to rid my thoughts of the swinish janitor and to open them to the decorous drama that was playing at the table. What I do remember quite sharply was when my friend began nipping at my sleeve.

"Bathroom," he said.

"You want to go to the bathroom?" I said.

"Bathroom," he said, still pinching my sleeve and tugging at it.

"Lad, lad, you can manage for yourself," I said, more amused than bothered, really.

We all watched him stagger off.

He seemed to make his way well enough—stepping uncertainly, but a sure bet to carry out his mission without assistance.

We watched him go around a corner and then we fell to chatting again. I believe I introduced the matter of the sled, an unspeakable theft, an outrage that would give me no peace. I must add that my companions seemed eager enough to discuss the matter, to register as yet another insupportable instance of the trying circumstance we urban dwellers are asked to tolerate.

"Vandals," I said. "A city of vandals."

"We live in fear of plunder," the other fellow said.

And the woman added, "No one is safe."


We were getting on rather briskly with the subject, I must say. But conversation suddenly ceased when, as one, we understood our host had been absent overlong.

Should someone go look?

The woman said, "Oh, it always takes him forever."

I recall thinking this her first coarse remark of the evening, and was a shade disappointed that this piece of tastelessness was likely as far as she would let herself go. The other fellow was on the point of rising when we all saw our friend appear from around the corner, stumbling in our general direction, but making reasonable headway.

When he had seated himself, the woman addressed him with a marginal smile. "It always takes you forever," she said, saying this clinically and not with the familiarity, on the one hand, nor with the hostility, on the other, that you might have expected, given the program that underlay our little assembly.

I believe I was astonished at how even-tempered the whole peculiar affair was turning out to be. In a way, the equable character of the evening was the least tedious aspect of it, one's assumption being that the expectable would happen. Yes, I had liked it for that.

She cries without letup now. But it is mainly at night that I catch her at it.

I have not asked her why she cries. Perhaps she does not know.

Besides, whichever of the few plausible explanations she chose, none would profit my knowing to hear. There is no surprise in her—nor should there be.

What the lesions left on my boy's face is exactly what I guessed they would. He picked at it—he could not keep himself from picking.

The landlord has sent a letter reviewing the procedure for the discarding of trash. He asks that I return to my customary respect for the premises. I will reply that my respect for the premises has not wavered. I will reply that I am unwavering in every respect.

I will reply that my boy will be unwavering in his time, and that my wife does not waver, either.

I wonder if it would disturb the custodian to know this.

I wonder what the custodian thinks.

I do not know how much longer we were talking and eating and drinking when my friend broke his silence to say:

"Didn't take me forever."

We stared at him.

"Are you answering something I said?" the woman asked.

Our host stared back, either past speech or not talking—it was difficult to tell which.

"Are you responding to something one of us said?" I said.

"Telephoning," he said.

"You were telephoning?" the other fellow said. "Or is it that you want to use the telephone now?"

"Telephoning," our friend said.

"You were telephoning," the woman said, "and that's what took you so long—am I right, darling? And who were you telephoning?" she said, her voice uninflected by teasing or annoyance, a mild voice and not without its charm.

"Wife," my friend said, tilting slightly forward with the utterance and then sagging back into his chair again. And then he slid all the way off it.

I happened to be nearest, and was accordingly the one obliged to hoist him from the floor and get him settled again. But the man was jerking me down by my jacket, and I suppose I was the only one to hear him. After all, he could barely speak above a whisper now. As a matter of fact, the others were no longer paying him any mind. Indeed, they seemed to have revisited the subject of urban evils, and to be exploring it with some passion.

"Sick. Come get me home. Wife," the silly tick said.

"Not *really*, lad," I said. "You say you called your wife? You told her to come take you home? To come *here*?"

But his only reply to me was more of the same.

"Wife," my best friend said.

I was ready when the bastard came. Doubtless, he presumed that improvising his routine would throw me off, his randomizing the weekdays and the hours that he cleaned. Certainly he could not have anticipated that I too could keep to an indeterminate plan, varying the time I departed for the office, the time I returned home, never repeating my behavior three days in a row. The principle was plainly revealed: it is the haphazard hunter who can track the patternless quarry down.

I was ready. I could hear him down there, struggling to climb the steps to the second landing, no doubt straining with the weight and bulk of the lumpish vacuum cleaner that he used. I had never seen the machine and I had never seen him, but I imagined that both were big—huge, perhaps. That is why I had the hammer in my hand when I opened the door to take up my station at the top of the marble stairs.

Of course he left off coming when he saw me.

He lowered the machine to free himself of his burden, a brilliant red canister very like a decorative oil drum, the thick white hose looped around his squat dark neck a colossal serpent that had kept itself hidden from sunlight since birth.

"What do you want?" he said.

"The sled," I said.

"Sled?" he said. "I have no sled."

He was not a big man.

I am not a big man. But he was not big, either—or so it seemed sighting along the diagonal line that ran from me down to him. And he was old. Sixty or more. In that neighborhood, I judged.

"You bastard," I said, and raised the hammer to make certain he saw I meant business.

"You're crazy!" he shouted up at me from where he with noticeable awkwardness stood.

"Crazy?" I screamed. "You call me crazy?"

I took two steps down.

He responded by shoving the vacuum cleaner against the iron railing and jamming it there with his knee.

"You're crazy!" he shouted again. "Leave me alone or I tell!"

"*Who* will you tell?" I screamed. "It is I who will tell! I will tell them that you called me crazy! *I* will tell, you filth! I will tell that you called the father of a boy crazy! I will tell them that if I am crazy, it is you that made me crazy! Filth! Dirt!" I shrieked. "Go get the sled from wherever you put it or I will give you this!"

I held the hammer higher.

He let go of the vacuum cleaner and it slammed all the way down, its sullen descent thunderous as the steel barrel bashed the marble all the distance to the bottom.

He was quick for a man of his years, huffing up the stairs with bewildering speed. I hardly had a moment to ready myself, to swing with the force that was needed.

I hit him. I hit him in the face.

It was a very heavy blow.


I had just got my friend upright in his chair again when the woman that was coming toward us called out. She called loud enough for everyone to hear.

"I'll take him!" she called, and all the diners turned to gaze, gape, wait.

It would be a scene that everyone could enjoy, the theater that is implicit in every public setting.

You know what I mean. We are all identical in this, too, in our expectation of disorder, in delightedly waiting for it to scatter the order that so astonishingly obtains. I, for one, am never impressed by the statistical increase in murder and assault, believing that whatever governs us and contains us and keeps us from destroying everything in sight has always worked a miracle against the natural scheme in human affairs. I suppose it is the task of breaking rhythm that so often checks us, our finding it ever so effortless to conform to the cadence commonly observed.

She came ahead, cutting a robust figure through the stilled tables, calling out to us as she came, "I'll take him! I'll take him!"

She would be the wife, I thought, and that is of course who she was.

I stood to make the introductions, and the other fellow, instructed by my courtesy, stood too.

"My name is," I began, smiling hospitably. But her attention was well to the side of me.

"I don't care what your name is," she said, regarding first her husband and then the woman who was still seated. "I want to know what her name is."

The second woman wasted not an instant. She pushed back her chair and rose. "My name?" she said, her voice no less moderate than when she had said, "No one is safe." I recall thinking what a wonderfully controlled woman this is, the very word of balance and restraint. I recall thinking what it would be like to enter her bed, to hear feeling expressed with such temperance. I imagined it would be a congenial experience, reminding myself that reserve nothing can dismantle is immensely more arousing than is the inner beast made manifest. It is this that buttresses my fondness for my wife.

"My dear," the second woman said, "I am the person your husband had been sleeping with until a few brief weeks ago."

We have a new sled now—not a plastic one, but a product made of a kind of pressed-wood material, a composite perhaps. Still, it is a Flexible Flyer, and that's the top of the line. We bought it the next larger size.

I suppose we would have had to give up the old one, anyway. To be sure, my boy is growing.

I wonder what sort of scar the custodian displays on his face. It was a ball-peen hammer and therefore the striking surface was round, a small knob about an inch across.

He still services the building according to some irregular schedule he has devised. But I have naturally returned to my usual routine, off and away at nine sharp, home at six on the dot, except of course for Fridays and Wednesdays, when I fetch the laundry and the groceries home.

You may be wondering if I have taken to placing the larger sled in the hallway where the missing one was kept.

I have, as a matter of fact.

I understand from my wife that the fellow still complains when he comes to do the carpet. He wants that little oblong cleaned just like the rest—and he says he will not resituate a sled to do it.

My wife tells me the old fellow is very angry about our persisting failure to cooperate, that he is threatening to remove any and all obstructions that interfere with his work.

The custodian says we are insane to continue to provoke him like this. That is what the man says—if you want to believe my wife.

# Guilt

*I felt adored. I felt adored by people and* things. Not loved merely. Adored, even worshiped. I was an angel, born an angel. I recall knowing I did not have to do anything particularly angelic to be viewed in this light. I was blessed, or I felt blessed. I don't think this feeling came into being exactly. I don't think it grew as I grew. I think it was with me right from the start. It was what I stood on. It was the one thing I was sure of. It moved with me when I moved. It was acknowledged by everything that saw me coming. Animals knew it, the dogs in the neighborhood. All the parents knew it, not just mine. The sidewalks knew it.

If I picked up a stick and held it, I knew the stick was holding me back, would be willing to embrace me if it could. Everything held me back or wanted to. The sky wanted to reach down with its arms when I went out to play.

I had blue eyes and blond hair and I was very pretty. I was favored in these ways, it is true. But I was not vulnerable on account of it. I mean, the condition of adoration in which I understood myself to be held was in no respect contingent upon prettiness. This was not an opinion of mine, not anything susceptible to test, proof, refutation by argument or circumstance. To say this understanding was conditional would have asserted nothing more than the testimony that life is conditional.

Of course.

Let's not be silly.


I wish I could think of a way to get speech into this without disrupting things. But I don't think I can. If presences could talk, I could do it. Presences are what counts in what I'm getting onto paper now that I am forty-seven. The people don't count. Not even Alan Silver counts. Besides, I cannot remember one thing he ever said. Or what anybody else said.

Here's what I remember.

I remember blessedness until I was seven. I was safe.

Then we moved to a different neighborhood, another town. The war was on, and I think my father was making money off it. He had more money, however he got it. This was a certainty, no speculation. In the old neighborhood, we were renters. There was some vague shame in this, being renters. I knew about it. The boys I played with must have said so, or their nannies must have. I supposed they were trying to interfere with the magic that encircled me. I supposed they envied me. Envy had been explained to me. I don't know who did it. I suppose my mother did. I suppose she warned me, told me to expect envy, to be ready for it, not to be surprised, to fortify myself, stay vigilant.

I admit it, it didn't work. There was shame attached to renting even if it was envy that inspired them to let me know that's what we were, renters in a neighborhood where everyone else owned.

Moving did not defeat this, though. What I mean is, between the time I knew we were going to move and the time we moved, I didn't fight back. I didn't tell the nannies we were going to own. I don't know why I didn't. I think I must have thought moving was more shameful than renting was, even if you were going to own.

Perhaps I thought we have to go someplace else to own. We can't own here.

I don't know.

It wasn't major.

That's how safe I was, how adored I felt myself to be, even by the nannies. Especially by the nannies.

I'm telling everything.

The nannies adored me because I didn't have one. This was a bonus. It was reverence on top of what I already had from them. The shame of renting was the same. It supplemented the universal blessedness. It was shame and it was intended that I be shamed by the knowledge, but it also abetted the well-being I was supposed to have. The nannies and the boys they took care of understood that my interests were secured, perhaps heightened, to the extent that humiliation was heaped upon me.

I understood this.

I understood it was queerly superior to be less well off.

I understood it was a good thing for me to be a child like this, but not a good thing for the grown-ups whose fault this was. The shame was really theirs. I shared in it only insofar as I could profit from it, be esteemed as more angelic because of it.

But then we moved.

The old neighborhood was old in relation to houses. The new neighborhood was new in the same way.

Houses were still going up.

You have to imagine this—a plot of land, everything dug up, mud mostly, three finished houses, five finished houses, seven finished, but everything still looking unfinished.

It stayed that way for years. Even after the war was over, it still looked like that.

They all had money from the war. This was what people said. People said it was war profits that got us these new houses. The maids said it.

There were no nannies in this neighborhood.

The maids were black and they didn't like the people they worked for. When it was only children around, the maids talked so that the children would hear them. In the afternoons, before they started getting the suppers ready, the maids stood out on the street near enough to where the children were playing. Profiteering was a word you heard because it came up a lot.

There was mud all over everything, every season of the year. In the old neighborhood, everything was finished and had a gabled roof or long dark beams crisscrossing over creamy stucco, turrets on the corners sometimes. And there was grass.

I'm telling you about the profiteering part only to show you how charmed I was. Let's see if you understand me.

Listen. Let's say I was seven and a half, eight, not nine yet. But I knew. I knew war profits was much worse than renting. I knew the maids hoped to put a malignancy abroad, hurt the children who heard it.

I heard it. It didn't harm what held me higher than the rest.

Alan Silver did that. It was Alan Silver that brought me down.


Here's what happened.

Alan Silver moved in. He moved in when there were seven houses and four still going up. He was twelve. Maybe I was nine by then. So that's the boys from two houses. The other five had boys in them too. There were girls, of course. All the houses had girls, but I can't remember any of them. Except Alan Silver's sister, but there's only one reason I remember her. Or one memory she's in.

The girls didn't count.

I can't tell you how much the boys did.

I was the youngest. Then came Alan Silver. The rest were older. But I don't know how old. There were five of them, and they were rough. Maybe they weren't rough, but I thought they were. This opinion derived directly from their attitude toward the mud. I mean, they played in it, or they picked it up and packed it and threw it at things. If they threw it at me, I went home and had it washed off. If they threw it at each other, they kept on playing.

They never threw it at Alan Silver that I ever saw. But I never saw Alan Silver play outside. I don't know where he played. Maybe he played inside. Maybe he went to another neighborhood. I never played with Alan Silver. I never talked to him.

But I saw him. Everybody saw him. Everybody talked about him. Not the boys or the maids but the parents. The parents said he was an angel. He looked like an angel. He had blond hair and blue eyes and was pretty the way they said I used to be—but he still was, even though he was twelve.

It was when I came across this opinion that I felt changed. I hadn't been noticing what was happening. I had been outgrowing my prettiness and I hadn't noticed. Isn't this amazing? To stop being the prettiest?

For the first time ever, I felt unsafe. For the first time ever, I felt they could get me, it could all come in at me, penetrate, kill me, find me in my bed, choke me and my parents wouldn't try to stop it, would sooner have Alan Silver instead.

I'll tell you how I handled this. I stopped going outside so much. I stayed away from where I might get mud thrown at me—and if it happened that I did, then I didn't wait around for it to dry first but went home right away to wash it off. This meant making worse tracks inside the house. So it didn't handle anything, because the maid yelled or my mother yelled or they both yelled—and when they did it, I could see them yearning for Alan Silver in my place.

I could see desire.

The way I used to feel the sky would put down its arms for me if it had them, I could see a heart emplaced in the air just above the roofs—a red, red heart.

It was desire. It was the desire of a neighborhood. It was my neighborhood desiring Alan Silver.


The first thing I heard was the siren. I was in the back of my house staying clean. Maybe the maid heard the siren first. Maybe she ran to the front door first, or maybe I did. But what I remember is the both of us at that door looking out.

The fire engine is up the block. By the time we are there looking out, the firemen aren't in it. Then there's screaming. But the maid and I stand in the door.

The screaming's from over there, over on this side, and

from this side comes Alan Silver's mother and Alan Silver's sister, and they're the ones screaming, and I never heard screaming like this before, except the time my mother did it, but it didn't last as long as this is lasting, because they're screaming all the way from over on this side to all the way up the block, and Alan Silver's mother is pulling at her hair, or maybe she's pulling at the sister's hair as they go running up there to where the fire engine is parked. Then everybody's running out of all the finished houses. They're all screaming and going to where the fire engine is, but keeping a little behind Alan Silver's mother and Alan Silver's sister even if they started out from a closer house.

I don't know what thing amazes me more—people pulling at their hair, or the fire engine on the block, or seeing the whole neighborhood outside all at once.

The whole neighborhood is out there where the fire engine is and where the firemen are coming out of an unfinished house, the very last one at the end of the block. Then they go back and then they come out and then they go back and then they come out, and it's then I notice the maid's not standing with me anymore.

My house is empty except for me.

They all went up there where something terrible was.


I went in.

I went back to the room where I'd been. I think it was the kitchen or the breakfast room. I went back to eating my milk and cookies again.

In the whole neighborhood, I was the only one who didn't go up there. Wasn't I too young to see a thing like that?

I knew it was a thing like that.

Days later, they started talking about it—the parents, the maids, but not any of the kids.

I knew in the doorway—or I knew when I was eating the food I went back for.

He lived in a coma for two weeks. But I knew he would be dead.

They said the five boys were playing with him when he fell. They said he fell from where the top floor was going in. They said he fell down through the shaft where the chimney was set to go—to the concrete they'd already poured for the basement.

I remember thinking, What was Alan Silver doing playing with those boys? I remember thinking, Was he always playing with those boys when I was staying clean?

Someone pushed him, I thought. I thought, Which boy did?

I wanted to tell everyone I didn't.

I am forty-seven years old, and I still want to say I am innocent.

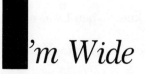

# I'm Wide

**M**y wife and small son were away for the week, having removed themselves from the day-to-day circumstance for a brief travel to a place of better weather. I was fine the first night, and remained equally fine the second and third, feeding myself from the cabinets and cupboards and pantry and doing what seemed reasonable in the way of tidying up. Yet each night I would put off my hour of retirement a trifle longer than that which found me seeking the safety of my bed the night previous—so that by the fourth night, it was virtually daybreak when I sought the security of blankets and pillow. Mind you, I was not passing the sleepless hours in any particular fashion, aside from the regularity of those few moments that saw to my nutrition and the succeeding clean-up of the premises. But I cannot tell you what precisely I was doing, save that I think I spent the bulk of the time moving from room to room and gazing at the objects that adorned them. At all events, it was during the course of the fifth night of their absence—of my wife and small son, I mean—that I was suddenly, in my meanderings, seized by the sense that I had happened to come upon the thought of the century. It was while staring at the seat of a wainscot chair of the Jacobean period, and while losing myself in the patina my week-by-week waxing of its surface had achieved, that I thought, Why wax? I mean, it was utterly throttling, this thought—*Why wax?* Why, indeed, wax anything ever again, when one could instead coat a surface with—*ahh*—shellac!

I was positively beside myself with excitement, gripped by a delirium of a quality I am not competent to describe. I remember thinking, My God, just look at me, an ordinary fellow abandoned by wife and child, now exalted in his possession of a piece of the most exquisite invention. I was quick to consider the fruitless labors of all those persons who, for years by the millions, had applied themselves to the rude practice of spreading on and then rubbing and buffing, this when one layer of shellac could end such oafish industry forever.

I went first to the shelves that we used for the storage of all inflammables, took what I wanted in the way of a can and a brush, and then made haste for my closet, there taking up the two pairs of shoes I then owned and carrying them into the living room, stopping en route to gather several sections of the Sunday paper from the stack it is our habit to maintain in the foyer closet.

Oh, you dopey goon! Did you honestly think it was the furniture I meant to have a go at? Great heavens, no. Shellac on wood has been done and done and done—whereas who'd ever thought of *shoes*!

I arranged things. I laid out paper. I pried off the lid of the can. I inspected the brush for dust, for hairs. Have I said that both my wife and son are endowed with hair of the loveliest colors? In any case, I went to work, and left my efforts to dry, sleeping more satisfactorily than it had been my fortune to do in years.

But when I returned from my office the following evening, both pairs of shoes were still wet—two nights thereafter (I was appalled), they were no drier. It was only then that I realized I had been wearing galoshes to my office in anticipation of the time I might return to the wearing of either of the two pairs of shoes I owned.

I went at them with a razor blade, the shoes, scraping. I scraped and then I tried a solvent. I admit it—this time I didn't bother myself with newspaper. I no longer liked the floor any better than I liked my shoes.

I won't make this last forever.

I murdered those shoes.

I hacked at them—I carved—I delved and delved, stabbing.

Towards dawn, I dumped them in the trash, and got out the vacuum cleaner to suck up the shards of leather. But I could see where there was no repairing the floor with suction. The solvent had eaten holes through the varnish. It was leprous, that floor. It was horrible.

I skipped my office after scrubbing off the stain on my hands. I went in galoshes straight to a shoe store, took a seat, and stuck out a galosh.

I said, "Nine-and-a-half, E. Give me a brown brogue."

"You mean wingtip?" the bastard said.

"That's it," I said. "E. I'm wide."

"In a jiffy," he said, and the purchase was made, the whole affair accomplished in minutes.

I was fine. All the way home, I was fine. For the rest of the day I ate biscuits and tidied and waxed those shoes. It was not until the new shoes seemed as shiny as they would get that I left off and squatted there gazing at things, studying the chairs and the tables, all those surfaces that gleamed. It was then that I was willing to reckon with the rest of what I'd said to that salesman when he'd asked why in the world I was wearing galoshes now that the streets were bare of snow.

It was then I was willing to reckon with the smile that had announced my answer. Oh, the words that so readily followed.

"Listen," I said, "I got this boy. God love him, he's seven, and all he wants to do is do for me. So what happens? When I'm not looking, what happens? Listen," I said, now widening that smile and raising my voice for the other salesmen to hear, "that kid, that wonderful kid, he takes a can of shellac to my shoes because he figures it'll put a shine on them that'll last as long as anything can last."

I even laughed when they laughed. Do you understand what I am saying? I winked my goddamn head off—me, a man.

# Imagination

X *was a teacher of story-writing, and* Y was a student of same. X was a remarkable teacher of story-writing. In the opinion of A to Z, exclusive of Y, X was the best there ever was. Still, Y sought out X for instruction—for although Y was not willing to hold X's skills in the very highest esteem, Y nevertheless held them in esteem high enough. Perhaps he viewed X's great gifts as a teacher as meriting X the status of second-best, whereas the first-best had nothing to teach Y.

Y was a hairy person, and very grave in his manner. X, on the other hand, tended toward the bald, and was lighthearted in all save two respects—his wife being one and stories the other. In these two matters, X kept up his purchase on the world as he thought it was, never cracking a smile in relation to either topic, a practice that Y thought foolish and tiresome. But of course Y had neither wife nor a vocation for living inside stories. Y wanted to write them, create them—and, as for women, he amused himself with reptiles instead.

Listen to X commenting on Y's stories, the which he judged the weakest among those produced by the class.

"What's this dragon doing in here? Why a dragon?"

"Dinosaurs are extinct. Write about the world as it exists in our time."

"Very good, except for the snake. The snake's a *deus ex machina*. Don't you see? You can't just stick a snake in there to resolve the conflict people have created."

X shouted. X was passionate about stories. In X's opinion, that's where reality got its ideas from. Y, for his part, listened with interest. After all, Y had sought X out to learn.

"For God's sake, man, why pterodactyls? Can't you make it a family of farmers instead?"

Y would smile. He had such a lot of hair and it all seemed to smile right along with his mouth. It made X think of Samson, all this ferocious growth, and of his own near-hairless surfaces. Poor X, his body was weak, but his mind, he observed, was very strong.


Then X met Z.

Oh, Z!

Z was neither teacher nor student of the writing of stories. Z cared not in the least for stories, and surely would take no position in the debate between X and Y. Z's enthusiasms were restricted to the parts of her body and to the uses that might be made of them.

How can it be that such a creature would come to fall within the ken of X?

In one version, Y proposes her, presenting her to X as Y's barber, the person whose attentions account for the vigor of Y's hair.

In a second version, X's wife is the agency through which X and Z meet, the former woman having heard that the latter can do wonders in the contest against thinning hair—restore growth, prolong life, work a miracle.

In either version, Z did—barbering X before and after his classes, a program Z kept up until Z's husband came back to her, thus making it necessary for X and Z to find another privacy for Z's talents to continue going forward in the matter of X's hair.

Insufficiency of it, that is.

Here's where Y comes into it again.

In one version, X and Y are quarreling about one of Y's stories, and X decides to give ground in order that he might then beg of Y a certain favor—in vulgarest terms, the use of Y's bed.

In a second version, Y remarks on the improved condition of X's hair, whereupon X, for whom everything is a story except stories that are not real, sees the way to make this one "come out," resolving the conflict that people have brought about, this without resort to some damned *deus ex machina.*

In either version, X and Z get Y's bed.

Or were about to, that is.

It was first necessary for Y to give X a set of keys and a caution, which latter was to vacate the premises before a certain hour, there being a cleaning woman and a delivery person scheduled to put in appearances at Y's at that hour in the first case and shortly thereafter in the second.

Did X understand?

He did.

It was not difficult for the teacher to be instructed by the student since, apart from the writing of stories, X appreciated he had everything to learn. On the other hand, that wasn't much—since, for X, very little stood apart from the writing of stories, the major exceptions being X's wife and now, of course, Z. And besides, Z only counted in what she did for X's hair.

In X's opinion, both before and after this story, he wouldn't have had any if it hadn't been for Z.

Now, in a good story, the reader would be entitled to know why. What was it that lay at the root of X's unlucky hair? Didn't X have a lady without a letter to massage his scalp, finger it with enriched shampoos?

He did.

In one version, this very question occurs to X himself— and in the same version, he is unable to answer.

In a second version, the wife is absorbed by her interests as much as X is by his, typing being the only one that really seems to grip her.

True enough, it was a means of supplementing the meager income produced from X's teaching. And anyway, didn't she also type for X—his lecture notes, his comments to students, though never a story he'd made up?

X did not have to make up stories. Those that were written for him to read and hand back were, in his opinion, quite enough.

"Be out by two sharp," Y warned. "Because the cleaning lady comes right on the dot."

"Good God," said X, unimaginative as usual, "you certainly don't expect me to let her in."

Y sighed in boredom with expectation coinciding with event.

"Of course not. She has her own keys," Y said.

"Two o'clock?" said X, wishing to make certain he was not uninstructed as to fact.

"Um," Y said. "She promised to be there in time to let the delivery in."

Now to the good parts.

Z was undressed.

Naked.

Not a stitch on her barber's body.

And she had carried it all into the bathroom to urinate and to place into position her device.

X, for his part, sat on the bed, his hairless flanks quivering with desire. Too, it must be admitted, with spasms of anxiety, set astir by what X now saw showing in the space between the floor and a certain closed door. Through the crack a red light glowed—a red light in a closet? Shining? Even an ordinary light would be something to think about— and X's brain went to work, invoking its powers to proliferate fictions, imagine stories, get scared.

A hidden camera? Maybe even a sound-recording mechanism too. Yes, of course! It's a setup. Y, Y, Y! It's revenge for all those criticisms, for "Very good, except for the snake."

X bestirred himself and leapt off the bed.

"Stay where you are!" X called to Z. "Don't be alarmed," he counseled manfully, "but I think there's something up," and with this X crossed the tiny apartment to fling open the menacing door.

X would have screamed had there been any life in him to do it. He threw his shoulder against the door and shoved as strenuously as a man with too little hair could. But the thing had its nose against the bottom of the door.

48

When it came to pushing, X was no match for what was coming out.

It lumbered sluggishly toward the center of the floor as X flew back to the bed, jumped up on the mattress, and flung himself against the wall.

That's how the cleaning lady found them—Z locked in the bathroom and X trembling against the asylum of the wall. It was she who got the thing back into the closet, where its feed was and its bowl of water and where the infrared bulb did its best to simulate the temp of its natural habitat. She just shooed it back in there with a broom, more startled of course by naked hairless X and the small shrieks borne from the bathroom than by the giant lizard that slumbered heavily in the middle of the apartment floor.

"It's called a monitor lizard," Y told X years later at a cocktail party celebrating the publication of Y's first collection of stories. "Dead now—couldn't take the climate. African, you know. Largest of the land lizards."

"I thought the Komodo was the biggest," said X, trying to put the best face on things.

"Well, you know," Y said, and turned to greet another breathless admirer, leaving X to doubt even his facts.

That story ends here. But this one goes on for a bit.

In this story, the end has different versions.

In one version, the delivery was a manuscript, and the person making the delivery was Y's typist—who is, of course, X's wife, and who arrives in time to see the cleaning woman gathering up the clothes eagerly anticipated by the man who is standing on the bed.

In another version, we have Y inscribing a copy of his book for presentation to his old teacher, X.

He writes: *Things always work out for the best. With affection and appreciation, your grateful student, Y.*

And then there is the name of the city—and the date, the first one.

# Frank Sinatra or Carleton Carpenter

*The man who stood, who stood on sidewalks, who stood facing streets, who stood with his back against store windows or against the walls of buildings, never asked for money, never begged, never put his hand out. But you knew that's what he was doing—asking, begging, even though he made no gesture in your direction, even though all he did was fix you with his eyes if you let him do it, and, as you passed, made that sound. It was *doobee doobee doobee*—or it was *dabba dabba dabba*.

It was always the same, and one or the other, but you never got close enough to hear which it was.

He was wearing high-heeled shoes the first time I saw him. They were women's shoes, or they were women's backless high-heeled slippers. I don't remember which. Yes, I think they were bedroom slippers—pale blue, furred, little high-heeled slippers.

I saw him the first week I moved here. I always saw him after that—it did not matter what the weather was. He was there in every quality of weather, backed up against a wall or a store window—*doobee doobee doobee* or *dabba dabba dabba*—Frank Sinatra or Carleton Carpenter.

He worked my neighborhood. I mean, he did what he did in my neighborhood.

I gave him a dime that first week. He took it. If he was not begging, then he was taking money. But I never gave him anything after the one time.

I was angry about giving him that dime. I felt it marked me as a sucker. I don't think I would have felt that had he not shown up again the next day, the next week, and every day and week after that.

Every time after that first time I always passed him by—*doobee doobee doobee* or *dabba dabba dabba*, oh so very softly—angry that the man was there, a witness to the fool I was.

That dime should have saved his life, gotten his back off store windows and walls, sent him away to another neighborhood, changed his song.

But he's gone now. He hasn't shown up for weeks.

It's a relief. I feel better about living here now—but it's not on account of that dime, not on account of the shame that I gave it and shame that I never gave another one after that. It's terror his absence relieves me of. It's the worst fear I ever had.

It was when the snows came this winter that I got very afraid of that man.

I want you to know how, I want you to hear how, the man made me so afraid.

I'd gone to fetch my son home from a playmate's house after dark. It was only eight blocks there and eight blocks back. But the snow was at its worst and there was no one on the streets, not all the way there, and almost not all of the way back.

We were three blocks from home, my boy and I, and the man was on that block, standing on the corner, his back to the wall of something. There was no way home without passing him or walking in deeper snow. So I went into the street.

The man just stood there—no gesture, no hand reached out. He didn't get me with his eyes because I wouldn't let him do it. But there was no escaping that *doobee doobee doobee* or *dabba dabba dabba*—just a whisper, really.

A car came skidding along the street. My boy and I were moving up it now and that car was moving down it, skidding, careening, a reckless driver playing in the snow.

I have such a childish imagination.

I thought: He'll hit us, that driver. I thought: My son will be hurt. I thought: There will be no one to help me, no one but the man I always passed.

I saw myself kneeling over my son. I saw myself begging that man to get help.

I heard him answering—*doobee doobee doobee*.

Or *dabba dabba dabba*.

Very softly.

Now that he has gone away, that can't ever happen.

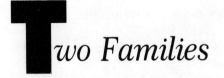

# Two Families

*There is no story in the sentences I will* write, no program to make matters come out. If matters do come out, then it is a resolution they accomplish all by themselves. No help is needed from me, nor is any solicited from you. All I am going to do—as briefly as fair play will allow—is give evidence. Everything else, if there is anything else, will take care of itself. In my opinion, it already has.

This concerns two families.

Families are families, and in this way are alike. But in every other respect, the two families that I have in mind have nothing in common. Of course, I issue this disclaimer mindful that its issuance disables it.

I cannot help that. It is what squats malignantly between writer and reader. But I have nevertheless done what I can to warn you away from speculations that will uncover nothing at all—though the caution will doubtlessly inspire the effort.

I want to answer that, but I am out of time.


In one family, there was a divorce. In the other, there was not. There was, however, in the latter case, a murder—whereas in the former, there was an attempt at one.

Let's begin again.

In one family, one spouse planned to murder the other. When the endangered spouse discovered the plan, he fled. He fled from one coast to the other and got a divorce. But up until that flight, he had stayed put. He said he had stayed put for the children. It was a good reason. There was proof of this when the children showed up damaged. They were very damaged. It will seem excessive to say it, but it is what both spouses said themselves.

"The light in them will go out."

When the spouses said this, they were talking about the happiness of children. But it may have been murder they were talking about. Who knows? I was never a parent.


There were two children in each of these families. As regards the amplitude, or the relative fall-off therefrom, of the light in the second set of children, the evidence isn't all available for recording yet.

But here's some that is. It is the declaration of the spouse that worried about the light.

This is what he said:

"My boy came to me, the younger one. The older one already knows. I never told him, of course. But he figured it out. Now the younger one has too. I love the older one more. I can admit that—it is all right if I do. Loving the younger one less makes it harder, however—harder about what he said when he came to me. He said:

" 'I know.'

"I said, 'What do you know?'

"He said, 'I mean about him.'

"I said, 'Him?' I said, 'What do you mean, him?'

" 'Why don't you kill him?' my boy said.

"That's when I knew he really knew.

"But I said, 'He's our friend.' I said, 'What a thing to say!'

"My boy said, 'That's what a man would do.'

"I don't know where he got that from, but my boy said that.

"Then he said, 'You're afraid. You're afraid to kill and you're afraid of him. It's because he's stronger.'

"My boy said all that, the younger one, the one I love less."

This spouse was afraid. He was afraid of the things the boy said he was. His boy knew that. His spouse did too. That's why she was not afraid to do what she was doing. That's why the man she was doing it with was not afraid, either.

They all knew where the fear was—especially did the spouse who had it.

But now it was worse. That father was afraid of that boy. He was even more afraid of that boy than he was of the other two things he was afraid of.

I think it was because he loved that boy less.

There was fear in the first family too. The spouse who ran away was afraid. That is why he did it.

The two children were afraid when he ran away. They thought everybody would run away. Bad habits of thought don't take much to get started. Well, that's when the light in those children began to go out. They were damaged, both parents were willing to agree.

They agreed on there having been some loss of light. But they did not agree whom to blame for this. So the spouse who wanted to murder in the first place set out to try it again. She would have to go from coast to coast to try it. But considering the greatness of her aim, the journey seemed no tall order.

She wanted to get to the one who would know all about how much light. You can see how she would.

She set out by car to do it.

Meanwhile—meanwhile in these sentences, not meanwhile in these events—the father of that boy called that boy back to him.

"I want to explain," that father said.

"You're a coward," the boy said.

"Give me a minute," that father said. "Don't be so quick to call a man a coward. I want to make one last appeal to you."

"That's what cowards do," that boy said.

But perhaps he knew this father loved him less. Children so often know. It happens when they say their prayers and must give a sequence to those they number in them.

"It takes a strong man to go along with a sadness," that father started off. "It takes a very strong man to stay put. It takes the strongest man to be a coward if his son has to have one."

How this came out of his mouth was not how that

father wanted it to. It was hard to get his point. He knew he had one, but that was the best he could do.

"It takes a strong man to kill," is what that boy said, and it took him no time at all to say it.

That boy was not all that young. But he was too young for the idea the father thought he had in mind. That was when the father had another one.

He went to the man his son said was the stronger. This is what he said:

"You're stronger than I am. Your body is stronger. Your mind is stronger. I'm going to tell you something. My boy knows. The big one knows, but now the young one does too. It's okay about the big one—because I love him more— and I think it's all right to say that. But because I love the young one less is what makes it really bad for us. I can't do what I'm doing anymore. I have to do something else. But am I strong enough to do it? You know I'm not. But you are. Tell me if you're following me so far."

"I'm way ahead of you," the man said. "You have to do something, but you can't do it. So you want me to do it for you."

That father liked this. He said, "What proof that you're the stronger! You see the point? Kill her for me. What is your answer?"

"I don't mind," the man said.

"You owe it to me—don't you think?" that father said as fast as he could, already compiling the sentences that would turn over his sly purpose to the son he loved less. It would test that father to postpone the tale of his irony. But he was strong. He could wait.

"I like it," the man said, "that complexity of reasoning. It's strong."

That father was at the mercy of clever sentences. He said, "But you were way ahead of me with it."

She took the children with her. She planned everything—
the same way she'd planned in the first place. But now she
had to use a map.

She marked off intervals, the mileage each traveler
would have to drive. But the family was one less than it
used to be. That's why the younger boy got the wheel in
Utah instead of in Idaho. He said his prayers when he got
it, and then he drove under a truck with sixteen tires.

# For Rupert— with No Promises

*I don't think I would be writing this story* if the facts did not force it. Actually, it's publishing this story that I do not think I'd be doing unless I had a very pressing— really an irresistible—reason. It is probably necessary to say that I always imagined such a reason would one day come along. But I imagine many things—and why this one has caught up with me and most of the others have not is only the way it is with luck.

Not too much should be made of it, I suppose. My brother's, actually—*his* bad luck. But I believe that when

I arrive at the end of what I want to say I might also arrive at seeing the bad luck mine too. That's what comes of imagining things. It is also what comes of making promises you never intend to keep—or, worse, which you do not keep but which you try to convince somebody (even yourself) you have.

I made a promise like that once. It was a long time ago, and the one who inspired the vow was a child. A girl in this case. It was my conceit to think that she would remember the promise. But I don't think she really did. After all, the year was 1944 and she must have had other things on her mind, there being a war going on at the time and her being twelve or thirteen or fourteen (despite a large opinion to the contrary, I am not all that much a student of children, and am especially inferior, I have often noticed, at pinpointing their ages), with all the calamitous worries that seize a child of such an age when its father has gone away. But she always wore a Campbell tartan and a watch much too big for her delicate wrist—and in those days in Devon and those days in my heart, a promise of any sort to a gentle child in plaid (with a weight too great for her arm) was not a thing I would not want to make. Besides, she had a little brother and always took good care of him, fretting if he were within earshot of a fact too awful for a small boy to hear.

At any rate, I promised her a story (I had wanted to be a writer then, and for too long a while thereafter I was one)—and some years later I wrote a story that was meant to appear to be the fulfillment of that promise.

Of course, it wasn't. A writer, especially the sort of writer I was trying to be, can't write stories like that—a pretty story when a child asks for one, a squalid story when *that* is the favor she asks. What I am paying for now is that I shabbily led her to believe otherwise. I wrote a story, a not very sincere story, nor a very graceful one (the years since demonstrate that the world disagrees with me in this judgment—but all I care about is that the story was mainly made up and is bruised by a very great fracture in its posture of narration), and when the piece was cast into print, I sent her a copy of the magazine sheets with a patch of paper pinned to the first page. I hadn't even the courtesy to set out my one sentence in my own hand, but instead typed the following, after a greeting that consisted of no more than the three lovely parts of her lovely English name: "I always keep a promise—I mean, p-r-o-m-i-s-e."

What I am paying for now is the lie I tried to get by with then.

I often read a Viennese logician who, I think, would go along with such reasoning. I think he would also go along with my reasoning that I am paying now for too much imagining. That is the kind of logic he favored when he lived.

It will presently be clear that I am, however, chiefly paying for my having a brother I love more than I love my silence. It will presently be clear that by publishing—and *only* by publishing—the little story I want to tell you, can I stop him from doing a thing he believes he must do. It is an act of extreme gravity, of extremest gravity, in all the spheres of spiritual prospect human imagining can consider. Or it is an act of no consequence at all. I am not certain. I am too overcome to rest for very long with a certain opinion. So I choose instead to do the safe thing—to put this story out for print.

All of this, I sincerely *promise*, will presently be very clear. One does not talk about what I am going to talk about, *and* talk in defiance of habit, unless one is utterly sworn to being very, very clear. I have sworn myself to the effort to let nothing interfere with clarity of the first order. Not even the sound of one hand clapping must be let to raise a noise along the straight planes of the sentences I am going to set down—but, reader, reader, how I can hear that one hand clapping now.

My brother was an actor until radio gave out. After that, he tended bar on Fifty-fifth Street and on Fifty-seventh Street, and then he went to Oslo and then he went to Zurich, and when he came home he came home with a wife, a Swiss, a psychiatrist, and in time she proved herself a psychopath. But the time was not soon enough, for by then my beautiful brother and my handsome sister-in-law had a son. They named him, I felt honored to learn, David, called him Chap, and that is what he is called to this day, seventeen years later, fifteen of which Chap and my brother have not, not once, seen one another.

There was a divorce when Chap was two, and his mother, not long after, set up practice in El Paso, reasoning aloud that Chap's asthma would be more manageable there—the aridity—reasoning to herself, my brother supposes, that my brother would be taught what pain feels like.

You have my word for it that my brother did not need the lesson.

You have my word for it that he did everything short of seizing the office of the mayor of El Paso to force his residence in that town, close to Chap, close to the largest love in him.

You also have my word for it that my handsome sister-in-law did everything short of hiring ruffians to strong-arm the father well beyond the city limits. It was easy, considering. The woman, you will remember, is a psychiatrist, and a kind of official therefore. And my brother, as you by and by will see as the facts are disclosed, was vulnerable in a very particular regard.

My brother—I shall call him by a different name here—
my brother Smithy would return to New York with a sick
heart, and when its sickening had worsened, he would go
back to El Paso to cry out at the gates of the city. My mother
tells us that these weekly, then monthly, pilgrimages went
on for almost four years and were then gradually abandoned
as the facts proved unmoving, unalterable, permanent. I
was living in New England then, kept in very random touch
with family, and—it will be no surprise to them if I admit
it—discouraged them from doing other than returning the
discourtesy. You see, at that time I was still dominated by
the pretension of writing, although I was well past the point
where I had fled from doing it in public. But, of course, I
did hear from my mother and from my sister—and when
Smithy had moved back to New York from Switzerland,
from Smithy himself—that he had taken a second wife, a
Swiss again, a woman somewhat older than the first and
anything but a psychiatrist. This sister-in-law, whom I have
not seen to this day, had banking as her profession, and still
has it.

I do not need to see her to know that she is handsomer
than the psychiatrist, for her photographs show up in the
magazines and in a newspaper that is regularly attentive to
very handsome and very active women, and my mother clips
and forwards every single picture through an agent who
has long given excellent service as an intermediary. And
Smithy, who telephones often now that I have devised a
truly private line, never fails to remind me that I am the
brother-in-law of one of the world's most admired women.

But I do not need Smithy's reminding, nor my mother's
clippings, to know how breathtaking Margaret must be—
for the child of her marriage to my brother I have five times
seen in the flesh, and he is the very word of loveliness, in
this as in all things.

The boy's name is Rupert—and he is the child of all our dreaming.

If I say more about Rupert in regard of his unearthliness, I will not be for long free from confusion. I will—what I want to tell you will—fall victim to the disorder of passion, and I have promised you clarity. I have also promised someone squalor. I now intend, with reverence and with haste, to keep both promises—and to save my brother, and everyone else, in the bargain.

Rupert will be five on his next birthday. That is the last I will say about my brother's second golden son, comma purposely omitted. The next voice you hear will be Smithy's, and I can make no boundaries for *him*. *His* italics are entirely his own.

"Stoke up a cigarette; this is going to take a long time."

"I quit smoking. Snuffed my last butt the tenth of October. If Mom would tell you *any*thing, she'd tell you *that*, and you promised me you were going to start *listening* to Mom, remember?"

There was a silence—not a good silence.

"Smithy? Hey, buddy, you there?"

"Please don't buddy me right now, Buddy. Please. And *please* don't kid around. I've finally thought the thing out, and what I've got to do—Buddy, *dear God*, I cannot believe I am saying this out loud—I am going to kill my son."

I did not shift the receiver to my other ear. I did not do anything that I can especially remember. I think if I had had a cigarette handy, I would have lit it. If there had been cigarettes in this house, I would have smoked them all. If I could have asked him to wait a half hour, I would have gone into town and bought a carton. Anyway, I did nothing—and I *said* nothing—because it was progressively occurring to me that I did not know *which* son Smithy meant, and that maybe *he* did not know either, and that if I said something which suggested one boy or the other, the suggestion might tilt my brother in one direction or the other.

Have I told you that my brother has twice *been away*? I know I haven't—because that is a fact that would certainly mislead you, and the one thing this piece of writing must *not* do is mislead you. But when one has a brother who has *twice* been away and who *married* a psychiatrist, one can oneself be misled by such facts. You cannot read enough of the Viennese logician to escape *certain* facts, and these may be among them.

"Buddy? Buddy, did you hear what I *said*? You want to go get a smoke now, big brother?"

And then he started crying, sobbing wretchedly. I had always imagined men could cry like this, but I had never heard it. It went on for a long time, and I was glad it did, because I believed that whatever had set it in motion would wear itself out this way and that would be that.

But it wasn't. Smithy stopped his weeping as abruptly as he'd started it, and when he began his first new sentence, it moved to its period with austere dispassion.

There's something else I have not told you. If he wanted, my brother could give the Viennese logician cards and spades. Smithy is very, very smart, endowed with an intelligence unsurpassed in our family and as statuesque as any I've come across. Moreover—and this is why I am not sure I am doing the right thing but only what I, like our Smithy, am convinced I must do—Smithy's unyielding custom is rationalism, all the way to the gallows if that were his destiny. There's never been anyone who could break him of that habit, and that goes for our older brother too—who could, just mentionably, break anyone of anything if he wanted to, and who would not flinch over breaking himself

66

into nineteen pieces to do it. Except Smithy of his rationalism, of course.

But our big brother never had a very long run at it.

Anyway, Smithy's next sentence, and all the sentences that rolled after that one and that I would not have dared to interrupt even to scream *Fallacy of the Middle!* were proportioned and stately in the chaining of their argument. And this is what my brother said—and why my brother has concluded that he must kill his son—and why I am publishing what the reader may apprehend as a "story," but which Smithy, ever the rationalist, will understand as a disclosure one step short of my informing the police and a step quite far enough to stop him in his tracks.

And, of course, the boy Chap will have his fair warning.

It is the least a loving uncle who has made his fortune (and his prison) writing can do. He can write as he is able. He can write a "story" that no one but the ones who most matter to him will quite be certain is true. I *do* see now that it is only through the miracle of the falsehood of fiction that I can catch up the people I love from the truth and consequences of what they might do. The cost to me is very slight in comparison—the exception in a habit for silence (Are you smiling now, dear dead brother, master of ceremonies in all my deliberations?) and the reinstatement, for a time, of the shame that covers me whenever I play the thief of hearts and come like a highwayman to the printed page.

*Speak*, Smithy! I am the instrument by which you may submit your supreme reasoning—and the dark circumstance that stirred it to unfold its awful syllogism. And when you have stated your case, I will return for a parting courtesy to the reader, a gesture I swear to be greater than that to which I proved equal when I wished to say the right thing to soothe that splendid girl of Devon. I am thinking I owe a very particular politeness to the reader—who, for the purpose before us, and as do his mother and father, I call Chap.

*Listen*, Chap. The father of your body is speaking to you. Will you recognize his voice? You were not much more than two years old when you last heard the peculiar American resonance that made your dad a regular on "Rosemary of Hilltop House" and "When a Girl Marries," a kind of choked vibrancy that must have softened when he blessed you to sleep and drew the covers to just under your chin, high enough that not one whisper of cold would chill your breast, but not so high that your restlessness would slip the blanket higher and close off the glorious song of your breath. This is the father of your body whose voice you are going to hear. Will it be at all familiar to you after fifteen voiceless years? Will it frighten you to hear a silence broken? Certainly the speech he makes will seem frightening—for it is a statement in support of his decision to secure your death. But it is, nonetheless, a reasoned argument, and if you are your father's son, Chap, you will see he has a point.

*Listen*, boy! A brother I love like life itself, your true father, on the fourth day of November, by long-distance telephone, just after the dinner hour, his voice as even as a machinist's rule, his heart an open field where two giants collide, said *this*:

"I have a pad and pencil here, and it's all worked out, that thing you know I do with columns, this on one side, that on the other. Buddy, can you grab a piece of paper and something to write with? I think it'll help—I think it'll help if you make notes as I go along. I mean, it's just that I want you to know how it happened. Most of it has been happening for years. I think it has always been in the back of my mind since Pert was born. Maybe even before that, in a crazy kind of way. Maybe it dates back to when I kissed Chap goodbye and could never get back to kiss him again. In any case,

I don't want you to think this *wasn't* among the scenarios that always go on in my head—because the head will *do* these things, Buddy—and you just can't stop it. Aren't you the expert in that subject? I'm rambling; I'm sorry. All right, I'm going to pick it up from what I've got *written* here. By the numbers, okay, big brother?

"About two weeks ago—hell, I know the *exact* day, who am I kidding?—Scharfstein told me I've got cancer. Wall-to-wall cigars and three packs of Raleighs a day for almost twenty-five years, and I get cancer of the goddamn *spleen*. I've always agreed with you that Scharfstein is a bastard, but his medicine is the best. Anyway, he sent me over to Sloan-Kettering that afternoon, and by the next morning they'd confirmed. Three to six months with routine measures, maybe another three to six with heavy anti-protein therapy. But that's it—that's tops.

"Maggie knows, of course. I didn't tell Mom or any of the rest, although I promise I will just as soon as I can figure out how I want to do it. And maybe you *can* help me with *that*. For the time being, all I'm doing is getting my life in order, squaring away my affairs, as Maggie would call them. Everything's pretty shipshape, actually—all the durables. There's plenty of money and there's nobody better than Maggie at managing. Then there's *Pert*—and that's, of course, clear sailing too. He could be the President of the United goddamn *States*, or change the theory of zero, and *this* won't stop him. My being dead, I mean—my dying. Pert could *be* anything, *do* anything. You know him; you've seen that for yourself. You just have to take one look at him to *know*.

"Except there's this one thing—and that's Chap. And if you don't mind, Buddy, I think I want to refer to Chap as David from here on out. There's David—*he's* the one thing. There's my son and there's my son—and *that's* the scenario. Are you following me?

"What David's mother has done lots of divorced women do—I know that. Except I think she's done it better. But I'm only guessing, of course—because for fifteen years the evidence has been withheld from me. Can you believe it, Buddy? With people who feel about blood like us? Not one word, not one touch, in fifteen *years*? Jesus God, the woman is a trained *analyst*. If she can unravel a synthesis, I guess she can ravel a good enough one up. Can you just imagine what she's probably *achieved* with that boy? It's not just a job of spiritual poisoning we're talking about—it must be more like a physical thing, the making of a biological system refined to a single tropism. Of course, I'm only guessing— but that's where my imagination takes my reasoning—and what else do I have to go on?

"I *believe* in David's loathing. Let's just say it's an article of faith with me—and with me dead, that loathing will logically transfer to *Pert*, don't you see? Loathing, envy, spite, you name it—and all of it susceptible to even greater intensity when David actually finds out what Pert *is*. I mean, what I see happening, when I'm gone, when all the rest of us are gone, Margaret and you and Mom and me and that woman—Buddy, I just *can't* say her name, not even now— I see a world with just the *two* of them in it: a peacefulness named Rupert, who owns all of my heart, and a man named David with a heart huge with rage. I see an empty place and my two sons—a hunter my existence made and a victim my loving put to sleep. What would Rupert ever know of what his brother must feel for him? How could Rupert ever *imagine*? No boy could—no boy like Rupert—and, Buddy, you know what Rupert is like. He is all light—a lightness, this one luminosity.

"Pert would never *guess*, even. But *I* can. *More* than that—I *know*. David will wait, he will wait his time—like his mother, he will be a creature of stark determination, patient, deliberate, a fury waiting for his chance. All right,

perhaps I'm imagining *too* much. Perhaps it will never come
to that—something violent, an injury, a killing, who knows?
Perhaps instead it will be a civilian act, but decisive, dev-
astating—David sitting on some committee which Rupert
happens to be petitioning, David behind the interviewer's
desk for some job Rupert must have, David installed at a
judicial bench below which Rupert pleads his case, David
standing with gloved hands while Rupert lies before him,
chest swabbed and bare to the scalpel—hell, I don't know,
Buddy, but I know it'll be *some*thing. Some way none of us
can predict, my firstborn will stalk my second, find a way
to hurt *him* because my death *robs* him of his chance to
hurt *me*.

"Look, there's nothing fishy in this, but I don't want
to talk anymore—and besides, I'm calling from home and,
with Maggie in the house, it's making me jittery—and I
right now can't chance being *jittery*. I'll telephone tomorrow—around noon—so for Christ's sake, *be* there. Because
I promised Scharfstein I'd come in and see him in the morning—the jerk thinks he can teach me how to die—and I
plan to fly up to Hanover in the afternoon. I guess Mom
wrote you that David started Dartmouth this fall—all the
way from Texas to my *brother's* backyard!  Buddy, he writes
these letters to his grandmother that I cannot believe and
*do* not believe—like a *geometer's* been at them. It gives me
the willies to see them, but Mom always makes sure I do.
He writes to *her*! Does he write to *me*? Does he answer *one*
goddamn letter? Anyway, that's where he is and that's where
I'm going tomorrow to get it taken care of. Jesus, man, I've
got to *choose*, don't you see—*and I choose Rupert!*"

Your father hung up, Chap, with the delivery of that declaration. I didn't wait until the next day, though. I called
him back right away—and this time I did get a piece of

paper and a pencil—for no good reason, actually, but in moments of this kind one sometimes does things like that. If you are your father's son, you will understand. I didn't say much. I didn't try to argue with him. I don't think I then knew what logic to argue *with*—and I am not certain I know that even now. All I did know was that I had to try to stop him—not because there was in me a conviction that held him *wrong*—but only because there was a will in me to stop him if I could. He did not answer right away, but when he did lift the receiver I immediately said, "Me again," and then I heard him say, "Mags, I've got a call and I need to talk in private. I'm sorry, but I need to," and then there was a moment's quiet and then my brother said, "Yes?" and I knew there was no arguing, nothing to do but state the livable range marked off by the mad reason of his assumptions.

"I have one thing to say," I said, "and that's this. Let it rest for three months. They've guaranteed you three months, at *least* three months, so you can wait that long and *then* do it. Not saying you *shouldn't* do it—just saying you can wait the three lousy months. Not that I think you'll change your mind—or that I'm trying to get you to—but just that you're in this position where you *can* add three months to Chap's life with no danger to Rupert. The minimum they've given you is the minimum you *can* and therefore *must* give Chap."

I was writing the numeral 13 again and again across the paper that I had pressed with the heel of my hand up against the wall. But the stucco was making them come out crooked, no matter how carefully I tried to control the pencil.

Chap, your father said, "Yes," and then he hung up the phone. He hung up without one other word. But the word he had uttered left no doubt—it was said so I would know there was no doubt. My brother knew that I knew he would do it—that your father would give you all the life he could.

That was the fourth of November.

I began writing these sentences that night, *last* night— and as I write this sentence now, it is morning.


I promised a courtesy, and this is it. I make this gesture to exist in the place of all the gestures I have not made. I am keeping every promise I have not kept. I am leading along to this courtesy everyone I have loved and ever misled.

There is an American writer, a woman, the only American writer I read. She has not written many stories, so it is no great undertaking to read everything she has written, which she has let have a life in print, that is. I take it that her public, unlike mine, is very, very small. This, I believe, is because she is unwilling to mislead, as I have so very often done and then tried to undo by my silence and now am trying still harder to undo by this last speaking up.

It *is* a great undertaking to understand even *one* of her stories, such as the one she brought forth into the world about two years ago. It is a story that will not stop. Its sentences (they are many) keep calling to my heart. The story began as a story that she had stolen from another writer—but only because *he* had earlier stolen it from *her*. It was *her* story, she said, and it had to do with magic and with miracles and with many, many things. I think it had to do with everything.

Near to its infernal conclusion, the story happens on the writings of a very wise man, a man now in prison for the doing of a crime. His crime was wisdom. His crime was knowing too much—about the weakness of man and the terrible power of God, never more terrible than in the offering of His justice.

Among these writings, as the story calls the wise man's

73

diaries, there is a tale the criminal has recorded. Here is the tale.

A father is in a concentration camp. He learns that the list for the next day's gassings includes the name of his son, a boy of, say, twelve. So the father bribes a German (a diamond ring, he promises) to take some other boy instead—for who will really know *which* boy is taken? But then the father is uncertain of the rightness of his plan. So he goes for counsel to the rabbi in the camp. And the rabbi will not help him. The rabbi says, "Why come to me? You made your decision already." And the father says, "But they'll put *another* boy in my son's place." The rabbi hears this, and he says, "Instead of Isaac, Abraham put a ram. And that was for God. Whereas you put another child, and for what? To trick the devil."

The father says, "What is the law on this?"

The rabbi answers, "The law is don't kill."

The next day the father does not deliver the promised bribe, and the Germans kill his son.

The father wanted a miracle, and he decided God would not give it.

But God did.

God created a father who could abide with the facts.


Oh, Chap, silent son, and all the beloveds I have promised, dear brother in heaven and dear brother still on earth, *this* is the one mir—I mean, m-i-r-a-c-l-e—there is. And you, Rupert, melodious child of our dreaming, for your birthday I give you this gift. It is the truth I have placed before you—for when you are five and must be strong enough for the five candles on your cake.

*Breathe.* Now blow them all out. Now good luck and long life.

# Weight

*The four things are a key, two benches, and* a bicycle wrapped in party paper but not where the handgrips and the foot-pedals are.

The key opens someone else's door.

The park bench overlooks a river.

The other bench is down where the subway runs.

The bicycle's a chimpanzee's.

The key is a duplicate.

The park bench stands in sunlight.

Four citizens are seated on the bench down here. The one free place is next to me.

The chimpanzee will speak for himself. But I say it's custom-made, the bicycle, balanced to the gram. See where the paper's split? That's chromium underneath.

The key is cut from cheap metal, a feathery replica of the brass original—lent, copied, seventy-five cents. It has no weight worth notice. Sometimes he does not know it's in his pocket. But it's there sometimes—once a week.

Of course, it's filthy down there, but it's also filthy up here. And the floor the chimpanzee rides on, this is filthy too—peanut shells, popcorn, gummy substances flattened out to ovals that are forever going to be sticky.

"I started on the bicycle when I was half the size you see. It's adjustable, wing nuts for all the crucial parts. I did not have the hat at first. But after one circle without a slip-up, I did. After four, the jacket. After eight, the trousers. When I could keep it up and keep it up—at least in theory— the shoes were what I got for it. They're sturdy. They're black. See the buckles for getting on and off?"

Now for people.

There's the man in such a hurry, hand in pocket, wristwatch raised to read the time. There's the couple in the park, the slowest pace of all, the bench they're oh so slowly making for. There's the woman down here marching back and forth. She reaches her mark, shouts, "Leather from Morocco!" turns about, marches back and forth.

You don't want to see her. I try not to. They try not to, the others on this bench. We are just passengers, persons waiting to be passengers. Oh, we really cannot wait to be. Will your train come before she does?

The old woman has the old man by the arm, to hold him up and steer. That's where they are going—to the bench in sunlight, to sit, to see the water—and the going is immense.

The man runs now, runs the last little bit, then puts

76

his shoulders into it as he hustles up the five flights of stairs. He takes his hand out. He takes the key out.

The marching woman shouts, "Handbags! Beaded handbags!" But there is nothing in her hands.

Oh, God, don't let her jump, not while I'm still here. Oh, God, don't let her want to sit, not while I'm still here.

*Sit.*

Is there anything else that this man wants?

It's been too long from the bed to the bench—and he is not there yet. "Up, my darling," she must have said. "Such a lovely sunny day calling such a lovely boy."

Oh, yes, that is how she, this woman, would talk.

"Up, sweet love," she must have said. "Come, my beloved, another look."

It must have taken hours to get him dressed. See how nothing matches? Oh, it must have hurt to have those clothes go on—in something, touching anything, living one more minute.

He has his clothes off. He tunes the radio. Goes away, comes back, retunes. He looks at the clock, looks again, puts his hand in a trouser pocket, takes out his wristwatch. He's learned—always take your watch off.

"I learned without the paper on. The paper's just for show. What isn't? I learned. They put you on, you go. Listen, I can go and go. But I don't have to. An even dozen is all I ever have to. The bolero and knickers, they're satin, turquoise with pink piping. I had to wait and wait for the shoes. But I could have mastered the pedals with them. Cut off my feet, I still could have. The hat? It's red. That's traditional. Black, turquoise, pink, red—some ensemble, Jesus."

I looked. Or one of them looked. It only took one look and here she comes.

Oh, Jesus!

Should I check my watch and get up? Perhaps I must

hasten to an engagement farther up the platform. But I am just sitting here, and she is, too.

Her beauty is impossible—oh, the back of her as she turns him by such considerate degrees.

"Sit, my love," she says.

He says, "You, dear, you sit first."

But I cannot really hear them speak.

When she sits, she is not crazy anymore. She sits primly, hideous ankles primly crossed. She breathes a small sigh and falls silent, just another citizen, speechless like us all.

He flexes the fingers on this hand, that hand, then all the toes. He looks at the clock, at the door, at the clock, at his clothes. There they are, all laid out for him to put back on—his turquoise knickers, his fine fitted jacket, his shoes.

But why bother with it all? Just the trousers, then—then open the door and go take a look.

"Buckle this side, buckle that side—even a horse could do it if he had a thumb. But the children shriek their approval. Yes, they like the buckling of the shoes better than the perfect circles. Yes, yes, the leather hurts. But what doesn't?"

No, she is not waiting for a train. This is where she is. Yes, it is because she has kept him waiting longer than she has ever kept him waiting, longer than any of them ever did. Oh, it is because she has *never* kept him waiting that he goes down to take a look. Is the buzzer broken? Does she stand there, five flights down, calling him and calling him and he is way up here? She stands there, nodding, pleading, saying, "Please, my beloved, sit now—please, just sit." Look at his fingers flexing. Oh, God, he hurts! Oh, God, she's going to get up—and do what? Jump? Just march? Five flights half-undressed? Is there nothing he won't do? "I can do anything if you make me." But no one is waiting, no one is calling, no one is saying, "My beloved, my darling—sweet, sweet love." She's marching, just marching, back and forth from mark to mark. "Why must they be children? How can children know what it takes to do this? Can children ever know what it costs to keep your balance? They think everything does—houses stuck on mountain peaks of crayon going up." "Leather from Morocco!" Just march, don't jump! Back up the stairs, begging God, the slowest pace of all. "No, sweet love, first you—sit, please sit," and so she does. She sits and says, "Now you, my love," and guides him down. He stands there at that door. Nothing in this side, nothing in that side, nothing in the whole wide world. "There are no pockets in my trousers. If there were, I would load them down. Put rocks in, put mountains in, just to show them what I could carry and still go on and on and on." He turns and turns, these mute revolutions, this blind persistence—shirt, shoes, fine little jerkin all locked inside.

I never had that duplicate.

Or a bicycle that fit my size.

Or the courage to stay seated when the worst came.

I have a wife. I have the ungainly weight of my love for her. I am the beast who can circle without letup. In theory. So far.

# Fleur

*H*onest to God, it's something, how a thing comes back, how nothing is ever lost. Look at this—the Strand, the Columbia, the Laurel, the Gem, the Lido. And that's just from the night before last, from when I was sitting on the toilet, urinating.

The Central. I almost forgot the Central.

These are the theaters where I went to the movies back in the days when you went every Saturday. That's what? Thirty-five years ago?

Also, I saw the large carton of Kotex leaning against the bathtub.

News to me they had a yellow rose on there, long-stemmed and photographed to make it look misty. So what's the story, they do this how? Gauze over the lens? Vaseline?

So how come I turned on the light? Or did I?

I don't know. If I did, maybe why is because of the kitchen.

Listen, I say the thing with evil is it's a time thing—whereas where you get your basic appeal with lust and violence is because they're not. You see a person stick a person with a knife or with a hard-on, it's the quick effect which gives you your theater. Let's not kid ourselves, impulse enacted with all good speed, that's what the eye likes. What the eye wants is something it can catch all at once. But evil, there you're talking about a different story altogether—because with evil, the mind's got to get into it, and the mind doesn't work that way. The eye does.

Be honest with yourself, this is why Aristotle didn't give a shit about evil, and was twice required to say as much. Not that I am asking you to see it as how I am bringing in Aristotle to back any of this up. Hey, with the proof that follows?

Go back to before when I was sitting on the toilet and saw the Kotex and the rose. Go back, say, fifteen minutes from that. To me asleep. To me out like a light. Which for me is an interesting exception, the case being that I am no great sleeper. I mean, even if you hear me snoring, I am probably not sleeping.

Here's the second interesting exception about the night before last—which is that I am not a nose-breather when I'm supposed to be sleeping, which the reason for is this. You smell things, right? (In your bed, what's to taste?) If it's not your wife, then it's the pillowcase—or, even worse, yourself. But let's say that whatever it is, it gets in the way—when the whole thing is to think a certain thought and work down into it—like a wood beetle, falling asleep inside what he's feeding on—even though I personally never really fall asleep.

Not that I think a serious thought, like the thought I gave you about evil. What you want instead is something playful, even crazy. It's the truth—the crazier the thing you propose to the brain, the more it's like a hammer knocking you cold.

Now, the night before last I remember exactly—I'm thinking they should invent a cigarette with negative nicotine and tar, smoke it and it sucks all that crap out. Naturally, I must have been mouth-breathing to keep from smelling things. So go explain this little packet of molecules that for an absolute fact it's my nose, not my mouth, which detects.

It's like a shriek—*coffee burning, kitchen burning, get up and go take a look!*

Here's the smell. You know the smell of what coffee smells like when it's boiled away and the residue's turning crisp and the stove's next? But even in my semi-sleep I know it's me that makes the coffee in my house. Are you kidding? Let her make it? Besides, now that I am smelling things, I smell her right where she belongs.

You can see how there is another interesting thing here, which is this package of intrepid vapor. Consider, all day long it's been poking around the house, a look here, a look there, but come three, four in the morning, hi, hi, hi, it's like a dropper's been directed all the way into this one nostril and there's this solitary dose of disaster—*Jesus Christ, fire!*

Think of it—the Brownian motion. God, I love that shit.

Stop to consider. Those molecules could have maybe been airborne days ago. Maybe weeks, months, what? Centuries, whole epochs even—coffee left on too long by *cavemen*, right?

So it's this interesting thing that gets me up and not the thought to go put out a fire. Think of it this way—you have to acknowledge the majesty of the physics involved, the incalculable odds, time giving you the horselaugh, and so on and so forth.

Here's the story. I just stood there in the darkness in the kitchen. The next fellow would have snapped on the light to check. But me, I understood—I know science, I know philosophy—Aristotle isn't the only one. Turn on the light, what? There goes mystery, there goes fun—the stove vacant, the porcelain spotless, everything in my house the way I want it.

I got milk and cookies. Eyes closed, mind open, I got milk and cookies and propped myself against the counter, nibbling and sipping—a box with a mouth, the thing that wants things inside it, the lid wide open, check?

Okay, I am a thing waiting.

Aristotle, are you listening?

I needed a new thought. I needed crazy. I needed the little bit of sleeping I get.

So what came was me and Izzy and Eddie and Mel. What came was from the days of me and them—boys, boys about fourteen, fifteen, an age in there, a whore Izzy said we could all get if we got her a bottle and had enough money. So I don't know—getting the bottle was even harder than getting the money was. But I got the bottle, and I did the talking when we got there. She said we were nice enough boys, and I said seeing as how she said that, could she see her way clear to shave it to six per the jump. She said okay, six per, round it off at twenty-five, but just blowjobs, a woman maybe fifty, forty, small and soft, this fritzy hair the color of gum.

Izzy went first and then me.

Then Eddie came out, and Mel said no. So I went back in instead of Mel.

That's when I got her to drink all the rest of the bottle, and when that's what she did, she was a mess.

So I came out and said we don't have to pay her, she'll never know. Eddie says give her half, and Izzy says what's this?

It was what they used to call a little black book back in those olden days.

Izzy says, "You see this?"


We took it. We didn't pay her. We didn't give her one red nickel.

Here is the conversation I remember.

I said, "I don't think we should have taken it."

Izzy said, "We'll look at it. We'll see the names in here. The guy which told me about her, we'll see if he's in here."

Mel said, "Suppose we call them and tell them they have to give us money or we're telling, all the guys in here."

Eddie said, "No, what we do is we call her and tell her it'll cost her to get it back."

I said, "That's terrible. We can't do that. You've got to see it this way—we didn't pay her."

Izzy said, "Wait a minute, wait a minute, I'm thinking. There's something here we're not thinking yet."

I said, "Give it to me. This is disgusting. You guys are really disgusting. The day will come when you will think back on this, and I am here to tell you right now, you will be ashamed."

84

So the thing is, I got it away from them and I went to her place, and I got her to give me a twenty to get it back.

Night before last I was sipping and nibbling and just being a thing that was leaning and letting all of this come in, even the part about how for all the time I knew them after that, I never stopped showing them who the disgusting ones were and who the nice guy was who took it and gave it back. Eddie, Izzy, and Mel—I'll bet they still think so. Then I tiptoed to the bathroom off the bedroom and sat down on the toilet and turned my head another way. That's when those names came—the Strand, the Columbia, the Laurel, the Gem, the Lido—and let's not forget the Central.

Look, I sat there urinating.

The thing was to stay ready to fall more or less back to sleep. So why did I turn on the light to see the big blue box and the yellow rose on it, the million-dollar decision in some genius's brain to make the whole deal hazy?

# Three

*Three things happened to me today. One of* them taught me the meaning of fear. Actually, these were not things that happened to me. They were just things that happened in my presence. I am not even sure how much of my presence was involved. Let's leave it at this—I was there when these things happened.

The first thing was the woman speaking.
You might want to see her this way—nice eyes, nice

hair, pretty face, those bones, good ones. The eyes are liquid, the hair chestnut, a barrette hiking a section up front into a flung-back pleated effect.

I had my eye on those bones as she talked.

She was talking about a lover of hers, the man's funeral. She said she rather enjoyed it.

She knew I'd known the man. Perhaps that explains everything.

He was a lucky man before he died. I am thinking of the things he saw—the bones of that woman from top to bottom, those eyes swimming, the chestnut hair after the barrette comes off.

What a lucky man, I thought.

This is what I was thinking while the woman was speaking—even when she mentioned the funeral and said she rather enjoyed it.


The second thing was the head in the subway car.

This happened on my way home, one stop still to go.

I looked up from nothing in particular and saw it coming from the far end of the car, a wheelchair and a small black man behind it, pushing.

I know I took a good look right from the very start. It was because of the wheelchair. It was because here comes a wheelchair through a subway car. But what kept me looking was the absence of someone in it. It was just an empty chair coming down the aisle, a little black man behind it, pushing.

I thought, He pushes that thing in here. He gets you to look at him doing it.

Then I saw the head. It was sitting perfectly upright in the chair. I mean it, a head, right in the center of the seat.

It was a black man's head with a bit of a black man's beard, and there was a neckerchief at the bottom sort of rakishly flared.

You will say I am crazy. But I know I am not. I saw. I heard.

I saw the mouth in that head open up wide just as the train came in to my stop. I know what I heard before that door went shut.

It was full-throated, deep-chested.

Only one line, but good and loud.

*Way down upon the Swanee River . . .*

Very thrilling, very theatrical.

The son of a bitch was a baritone!

The third thing was I went home.

# Imp Among Aunts

*I threw one away just before I started this.* I tried and tried. But it wasn't any use. This one here has the same title that other one had because that other one had it. In that other one, I was telling the truth, which is why it wasn't any use. The only lie was the title.

But I don't want you getting off on the wrong track until that's where I want you getting. So just for the record, I did have aunts and I still have some of them, and I was always as much of an imp as I could manage.

They called me one, for that matter—the aunts did. Or they called me bandit or Mr. Mischief or rascal.

Bandit was actually *bondit*, which is another language and maybe doesn't mean bandit. But I always thought it did, even though the aunts put all their stress on the second syllable. Can you hear how that sounds? It's the truth.

I always thought so many things.

I was trying to get one of them declared in what I was writing and gave up on. But I just couldn't not tell lies about it, it being something about Aunt Helen.

Here's what I was doing.

I started off by naming all the aunts—like this: Ida, Lily, Esther, Dora, Miriam, Sylvia, Pauline, Adele, Helen, with Helen coming last, just the way you see it here.

That wasn't a lie but it was the beginning of one.

Then I got worse. For pages and pages, I said something bizarre about each of them—about the aunts—only nothing about the one that really mattered.

I'll give you an example.

I said, Take Dora. I said, Dora makes brisket and then goes to all the windows. There's Dora, I said, standing at each window, looking out of each window, going *oy* at every one. Just listen to her as she lets it go. Like this. *Oy*.

As for Helen, I was getting to her. I wanted to move up to Helen slow. Helen's hard. She's my mother's side. I wanted to move up slow on Helen, not get nervous doing it—because with Helen you could.

Helen could get you scared.

Here's what she looks like. Chinese-y eyes. Silvery hair. In a bob.

Helen was a spy. Helen broke codes. Helen ran the cryptanalysis unit at somewhere so secret you could die.

This is true.

I went to see her once. If I told you the state she was in, I might be giving away something too secret—so I won't tell. Of course, I don't mean state like emotional. State geopolitical is what I mean. Helen was never in a state emotional. That's the thing about her—the truth—and it still is.

Anyway, to get back to it, I went across the country to get to her. The place wasn't much, the apartment Helen was in. I suppose she was in it to be near where she did her code-breaking, the spying being all over with when the war was over and I got around to Helen again.

There was a buzzer, not a bell. That'll give you an idea of how crummy that apartment was.

The door opened a bitsy crack.

"Yes?"

"Aunt Helen live here?"

"Helen who?"

"My aunt Helen."

"Stand back."

I took a step away. The door opened a bitsy bit more.

"Who are you?"

"Her nephew. Are you Aunt Helen?"

"Say her name again."

"Helen?"

"Say yours."

"Mine?"

"Let him in!"

That was Helen, that last voice you heard. You would know it in a flash, scratchy and different, but with a cheeriness in it that was Helen all the way.

When the door was all the way open, you saw that it was a woman. She was really good size. She had a WAC uniform on her and a heavy automatic pistol stuck down in a holster strapped at her waist.

That's true—except it wasn't really stuck down. It was sitting in there—loose.

Helen stayed right where she was, back behind the

big woman at a pink Formica table with a pencil in her hand. When I got up close enough, I could see it was a crossword puzzle Helen was working on—slanty eyes, silvery hair bobbed to beat the band.

Oh, Aunt Helen.

She just picked up and left it all. I mean, in 1938, she just picked up to go be a spy and later on a code-breaker. She is famous with people like that—and with me, of course.

But I don't know another thing about her.

She's not talking.

I've seen her five times and she's never talked, not once.

She took me to the Russian Tea Room twice—in the '40s one time and in the '50s another. In the '60s they told her to retire.

She took a drive when they did. It took her through the state I was in, so she stopped off at my place to say hi.

But Helen still wasn't talking, not then nor ever.


I got to see the medals and the citations and the other things they gave her. That was in the '70s and in a different state from either of the two that have been coming up so far. It was the state Helen went to so she would have a nice place.

To get old. To keep your hair going in a bob.

Most of my aunts have gone to the same state—and they were ordinary aunts, just like yours.

That's another thing I wanted to tell the truth about in the thing I threw away—how it was the same state that finally got the ordinary aunts and the special one, the one I'm calling Helen.

I just did that to throw you off. Helen is her real name. But because I did that, now you'll never know. Not for sure.

There is no fixing it once it's done.

Mr. Mischief.

It's why I can write what I'm writing now and couldn't write what I was writing then.

Rascal.

It's why I can't write.

*Bondit.*

It's why there's never no declaring ever.

But you're looking at this and thinking these are really truths. You're thinking why make sentences if all they do is fool.

I am such an imp.

Every inch, pure Helen.

Go ahead and break it.

# The Psoriasis Diet

*I don't know about your first lesion, but let* me tell you about mine. It was just itching when it started, just a tiny itching place, a little dot is all. My mother said it was a bee-sting or something like that which got me. It wasn't. But everybody said so right up to the time it got as big as a dime, and then they all said if only it was a dime again. Because it wasn't long before it was a quarter and a bigger quarter and then a half-dollar.

*Psoriasis.*

I've seen worse words. Besides, it got me an education, being as how I took up an interest in language right after.

I started with all the pee-ess words and just kept on after that. There was no stopping me, I can tell you.

There was no stopping it, either.

They did everything, my mother and father. You can't say they didn't try. They tried all the things the neighbors knew about. Then they sent away for more. I put them all on. But you had to have a lot of stuff, being as how it was everywhere by now.

There was nowhere that it wasn't.

I was twelve.

I stayed home, as you can see—working on the dictionary. I just went on from all those pee esses to the rest of the trick spellings. I liked the old words too. Here are some of my favorites. *Pinguid. Pilous. Anachorism*, which I'm always getting corrected on. But this is the one which isn't about time.

I went to doctors when I couldn't stay home. They stuck me in a room. They got the clothes off me and took a look. They didn't like it, I can tell you, though they did their best not to let on.

I'd get a jar to go home with. It wasn't enough for the whole thing, of course. But they said the idea was to try it on a little spot and see how it goes.

The thing of it was, there wasn't any little spot to try it out on, being as how it was all one big one. Who could pick a place to stop at? I mean, where did you draw the line? It was the same thing with the dictionary, I noticed. You start with *paraplegia* and you go right to *paraselene.*


They tried everything. I wouldn't want to tell you what they tried. They probably tried it on you too, and it didn't work, did it?

I just went from sixteen to twenty-four—by which adulteration, I was bigger—and it got bigger too therefore.

95

You might say, we reached our growth at the same time. It was isochronous, you might say. That's if you had a vocabulary as powerful as mine.

I was on my own then. I can see how this was best for all concerned, being as how my folks just could not look at it and me anymore. To tell you the truth, I didn't look much, either.

I guess you know all about that part of it—the cathexis you get for always looking parallax to a mirror or not looking at all. Everything is askance, the way you see it—and I didn't shave, anyway. What's hard is getting the stuff from the jar on but never seeing where it's going.

You can do it. Anybody can when he has to.

But I'm not here to bellyache. What I'm here for is to give you the cure.

It's a diet. It's what cured me and it's what'll cure you—so long as you follow directions to the letter.

Here goes.

*Eat your heart out, sucker!*


If you want copies of this diet for your afflicted friends and relations, just remember I am protected by the copyright laws. It took me a lifetime to adumbrate my diet and I can't just go giving it away for free.

But maybe you don't want the cure. Maybe you really don't crave salutary skin. Maybe you'd be lonely without what you got. Maybe it gives you a conversation piece. Or maybe you just knocked wood that you didn't come down with Siamese twins.

I can understand that. Some people just don't want to be worse off. I didn't, either, until I decided I was.

Not anachronism.

*Anachorism.*

Look it up.

# **H**ow to Write
## *a Novel*

*F*<small>*irst make sure you have enough time. It is*</small>
crucial that you have enough time to make things up. I do
not have enough time for that. I don't have enough time
for anything.

I'll just tell you what's what. It will not be hard to follow. I am just sitting here and doing this, wasting time I
don't have.

The only thing to worry about is how much ground
you cover. But I'm too careful for that.

Just watch.

I'm composing this novel on an IBM Selectric. I got it

back in 1961. I did not buy it. I finessed it or I finagled it or I stole it.

The man that bought it was rich. He said you can borrow this thing, use it for a while. Then he stuck his other thing in my wife's thing. They still have their things and I have this.

It's given tip-top service. I really loved it when I first saw it, and I still love it just as much.

I never cover it over with anything. I don't cover it over because I like to look at it—the shape. IBM gives a thing a nice shape. I always look at it last before I snap off the light in this room.

I think 1961 was the Selectric's first year.

I talk to engineers whenever I get a chance. I don't mean the kind that build bridges. I mean the fellows that service things. Those are the engineers I talk to.

One of those fellows once told me buy the first of whatever it is—so long as whatever it is represents a significant technological change. He said buy the first because the maker builds extra into that one—just to enhance the acceptance of change.

That's why this one's still going fine after so many years of service. Not a single breakdown to this day.

I mean, I think that's why.

The same goes for the Polaroid camera I had. I had a really old one. They called it the Polaroid Land Camera.

My dad gave it to me.

Actually, no. I think I just took it once and never gave it back.

But it was a first one—the very first year they put the thing out.

It took pictures that sharp. Those little ones. But I could take those little ones and get them blown up that big and never lose a jot. I mean, whatever the resolution thing is exactly, that's what I wouldn't lose any of.

I took pictures of my second wife with that camera—pictures, pictures, pictures. I took pretty good ones. Then had them blown all the way up. They're framed all over the walls of this house. People come and look at them and smack their heads.

My God, they say, such pictures.

I say, original issue, stick with the first of a kind.

# Fear: Four Examples

*My daughter called from college. She is* a good student, excellent grades, is gifted in any number of ways.

"What time is it?" she said.

I said, "It is two o'clock."

"All right," she said. "It's two now. Expect me at four—four by the clock that said it's two."

"It was my watch," I said.

"Good," she said.

It is ninety miles, an easy drive.

At a quarter to four, I went down to the street. I had

these things in mind—look for her car, hold a parking place, be there waving when she turned into the block.

At a quarter to five, I came back up.

I changed my shirt. I wiped off my shoes. I looked into the mirror to see if I looked like someone's father.

She presented herself shortly after six o'clock.

"Traffic?" I said.

"No," she said, and that was the end of that.

After supper, she complained of insufferable pains, and doubled over on the dining-room floor.

"My belly," she said.

"What?" I said.

She said, "My belly. It's agony. Get me a doctor."

There is a large and famous hospital mere blocks from my apartment. Celebrities go there, statesmen, people who must know what they are doing.

With the help of a doorman and an elevator man, I got my daughter to the hospital. Within minutes, two physicians and a corps of nurses took the matter in hand.

I stood by watching.

It was hours and hours before they had her undoubled and were willing to announce their findings.

A bellyache, a rogue cramp, a certain unspecific seizure of the abdomen—vagrant, indecipherable, a mystery not worth further inquiry.

We left the hospital unassisted, using a chain of tunnels in order to shorten the distance home. The exposed distance, that is—since it would be four in the morning on the city streets, and though the blocks would be few, each one of them would be dangerous. So we made our way along the system of underground passages that link the units of the

hospital until we were forced to surface and exit. We came
out onto a street with not a person on it—until we saw him,
the young man who was going from car to car. He carried
something under his arm. It looked to be a furled umbrella—
black fabric, silver fittings. But it could not have been what
it looked to be—it was a tool of entry disguised as an umbrella.

He turned to us as we stepped along, and then he
turned back to his work—going from car to car, trying the
doors, and sometimes using the thing to dig at the windows.

"Don't look," I said.

My daughter said, "What?"

I said, "There's someone across the street. He's trying
to jimmy open cars. Just keep on walking as if you don't
see him."

My daughter said, "Where? I don't see him."

I put my daughter to bed and the hospital charges on
my desk, and then I let my head down on the pillow and
listened.

There was nothing to hear.

Before I surrendered myself to sleep, there was only
this in my mind—the boy in the treatment room across the
corridor from my daughter's, how I had wanted to cry out
each time he had cried out as a stitch was sutured into his
hand.

"Take it out! Take it out!"

That is what the boy was shrieking as the doctor worked
to close the wound.

I thought about the feeling in me when I had heard
that awful wailing. The boy wanted the needle out. I suppose it hurt worse than the thing that had opened him up.

Then I considered the statement for emergency services, translating the amount first into theater tickets, then
into hand-ironed shirts.

**T**wo

# For Jeromé—with Love and Kisses

*Jaydeezie darling,*
*dear cutie fellow,*
*my wonderful son Jerome,*

You will do me a favor and answer me this question, please God it should not be for you too much trouble to do it. So you will take all of two seconds and you will tell me, Jerome, since when did you hear of a civilized person which gets rid of a perfectly good unlisted and then goes and gets another one on top of it? Also, darling, assuming you could see your way clear to fit it into your busy schedule, you will inform me as to the whys and wherefores of how come the same aforementioned individual couldn't exhibit the simple courtesy to first communicate to his own father the particulars with regard to the necessary digits. So this is asking too much, Jerrychik? I mean, first and foremost your father wants your assurance he is not causing you too big a perturbance. Listen, you will be a sport and you will take all of two seconds and you will list for me the reasons for this behavior. Because to tell you the truth, pussycat, in my personal opinion, I think your father is entitled to hear an explanation.

I am waiting, darling. God willing, you will go into private conference with your heart of hearts and think the whole thing over and advise me as to your decision. So you could do this for me, cutie fellow? Because I your father am meanwhile sitting here on pins and needles expecting. Make yourself a promise that in a voice which is calmness itself you will pick up the telephone for the sole and exclusive purpose of advising I your father whether you decided in your mind if this is the behavior of a civilized person.

Meanwhile, who could help himself but to think along the lines of a certain possible conjecture? So plunge a dagger into my breast for giving serious consideration to the following theory, but are we dealing here with a situation where the party of the first part says to himself, "The phone rings and I pick it up, it could be the party of the second part trying to communicate with me, but could he do it if I get another new unlisted?"

So go ahead and plunge a dagger, Jerome, because what your father just told you is more or less along the lines of your father's personal thinking. And may I inform you, darling, that the father who is doing this thinking is also the same father who two seconds ago only wanted in his heart of hearts to say hello to you and wish his cutie fellow Happy High Holidays?

Sonny boy, I will tell you something. You got my permission to stab me in a vital organ for passing comment, but I want you to hear with your own two ears my appraisal of the foregoing situation. Because the answer is it's not nice. Jerome, when I see behavior like this, I have to say to myself it is not nice. And thank God I still got the strength in my body to say it. But don't look at *me*, Jerome—because your father did not make the rules, even if the rule is it is definitely not.

And so long as we are discussing the philosophy in this particular department, Jerome, I will tell you something else. Objectively speaking, in my personal opinion your whole area code should be ashamed of itself to have an operator that's got the unmitigated gall to say to a senior citizen get lost. Because in so many words, darling, this is just what the snip up there in 603 said. For shame, Jerome, for shame! And to a person of your father's years and age.

Are you listening to me, darling? To your own flesh and blood, a total stranger says get lost! So tell me, boychik, this is what they teach them in your area code? Or did this person get some coaching from a mutual party of our acquaintance who at this juncture I your father will leave unnamed? In so many words, take a walk? I want you to tell me, Jerome, what kind of a creature says take a walk to the father of the child? Because I hope I do not have to remind you that the father who heard these words said to him is also the same father who would lay down his life for his cutie boy, please God I should only be alive and well to do it when you got nothing better planned and you decide in your mind it is time to ask.

Look, darling, if God makes a miracle and you find the strength to call me, who knows, maybe you could afford to take an extra two seconds to give me the figures on what it costs you in so many dollars and cents to get an operator to talk like this to a person of my advanced years and age, never mind if I told her it was an emergency and also that the party in question is also my very own child. Listen, would the woman divulge the first digit? You are down to her on your hands and knees, but is this a normal area code with a single shred of human decency?

Boychik, I am sitting here and I am thinking certain thoughts to myself. So are you interested in the nature of your father's current thinking? Because the answer is if a certain person wants to be a hermit, well and good—then let him go live where they don't have an area code to begin with. But barring this contingency, I say that so long as you continue to maintain your permanent residence in 603, I think that I your father have a perfect right to be informed as to the rest of the particulars after these three digits!

Tell me, darling, did you ever stop to consider all of the ramifications of the situation we are dealing with here? So stop to think and tell me what if, for instance, it was a question of in sickness or in health? I want you to think about this, Jerome. I want you to consider it very carefully. They come in here and they shoot your father in the head. So like any normal person, I rush to the telephone to call you up and tell you the news. But what is the upshot in the situation we are considering? What is in this case the net result? Believe me, your father didn't have to go to college to describe to you what you get when you look at the net result. Because the answer is it's some snip up there in 603 which says to me when I am bleeding to death in so many words get lost!

Okay, so don't excite yourself, Jerrychik.

I promise you, all is forgiven, all is forgotten. And besides, it was only for the sake of argument I said it could be a question of in sickness or in health. So far they didn't come in here yet and shoot me. All right, you never know, but so far they didn't. Meanwhile, thank God it was only a question of hello and good-bye, my sonny boy should live and be well. I give you my written guarantee, Jerome, this is all your father had scheduled for the agenda, Happy High Holidays and hello and good-bye. In two seconds flat, the whole deal would have been over and done with, and you would have lived to tell the tale.

So go pick up a hammer and bang me on the head with it because your father was going crazy to hear his sonny boy's voice. Cutie guy, you know what? I only hope and pray I am alive to see the day when vice-versa is the case. Please God, Heaven should make a miracle and your father should live that long, you won't have to worry, his number is in the book. Believe me, you would not have to talk yourself blue in the face, Jerome. You would not have to stand on your left ear and dance a jig and then hear my particular area code say to my son, "That's cute, that's nice, now do us a favor and go take a walk."

So what is it now, darling?

First, it was your own room.

Next, it was your own business.

So now, in the final analysis, season after season, it's what?

Sonny boy, can your father give you a piece of his personal advice? You promise you wouldn't excite yourself if your father talks to you from the bottom of his heart of hearts? Because I am here to tell you, darling, sometimes your father does not know if he dares to open his mouth with you. But who can breathe with this on my chest, such a burden it's like a big stone? So go get a hammer and hit me with it, but meanwhile it is on your father's chest and he's got to get it off.

Sweetie boy, you know what it means where it says enough is enough? It means you do not go overboard! It means whatever the department, it gets handled accordingly. Because there comes a time in every life when enough is definitely enough. And you know something? Your father did not have to go to college to tell you this is the rule. But go look it up for yourself, it's there in black and white. You name me the department, the answer is you don't go overboard because the rule is enough is enough. Like with the woman who goes up to the judge, for instance, you heard about this, Jerome? So this woman says to this judge, "You'll give me a divorce," and the judge says back to her, "At your age you want a divorce? You are how old, ninety, ninety-five?" And the woman says to him, "Ninety-seven last July." So the judge says to her, "You come to me now, ninety-seven last July?" You hear this, Jerome? That judge says to this woman, "Why come to me now, a person who could any instant drop dead?"

Jerome darling, I want you to know what this woman said to this judge. Sweetheart, are you listening with both ears? She said to this man, "Because enough is enough."

This is wisdom, darling. I don't have to tell you, this is wisdom. Granted, you are a genius in your own right. But even a genius could live and learn. Even a brilliant man like that judge could. Believe me, Jerrychik, that woman didn't have to go to college and study at the feet of no Einstein to teach that judge what it's all about. And the man was an educated man, Jerome. But just ask yourself, did the man or did the man not have a lot to learn?

Boychik, this is your father's advice to you from your father's heart of hearts. In words of one syllable, darling, there comes a time when you have to say to yourself enough is enough. But let's face it, who am I to open up my mouth and try to teach a genius like yourself? Listen, just because I am the father and know from bitter experience, does this

make me entitled to tell you what it's all about? Forget even
that I am the elder, Jerome. Forget even that I as your father
would jump off the highest building for you. It still doesn't
give me the right to come along and spell out the facts of
life for a person who is a genius, even if it just so happens
he doesn't know which end is up.

But meanwhile, boychik, your father knows what he
knows, and he didn't wait around for some professor to come
along and spell out the facts of life. You name me the subject, Jerome, every college in the world will tell you there
is one rule that is first and foremost, and for your information
it's the one which says enough is definitely enough. Granted,
a genius has a perfect right to think to himself, "I am a
genius and I just discovered a subject where the rule is
enough can never be enough." You think your father doesn't
understand this, Jerome? You think your father doesn't realize that with a genius the brain gets all balled up and it
says to itself, "I just found a subject where all bets are off"?

So just for argument's sake, sweetheart, let's consider
this particular situation. Because your father is willing to
go along with you and consider the question from all sides.
Like just suppose I pick a subject off the top of my cuff and
we go ahead and examine it like two civilized adults. So
how about for instance PRIVACY maybe? Let's for instance consider a person who says to you he has got to have
his PRIVACY or else. So for two seconds, Jerome, you
and your father will make believe that this is our subject,
P-R-I-V-A-C-Y.

Now tell me, darling, did your father know the one to
pick? Because don't worry, Jerrychik, this subject your father
could put his hands on it for you *blindfolded* even with his
eyes shut and the room is pitch-black. Not to mention he
could also spell it for you backwards and sideways and
meanwhile tell you it still comes out the same thing, which
is G-E-T L-O-S-T. But God forbid your father should dare to

start to spell for a person who is a genius and is supposed to know how to spell for himself.

Listen, pussycat, you don't have to stand on ceremony with me, I promise you. Go ahead, whenever you're ready, I'm ready. Go get a hammer or a dagger, whichever it wouldn't be too big of an effort for you to get. Believe me, sweetheart, as a genius and as a brilliant child, you got a perfect right to go ahead and get whatever pleases you. I say God willing you could even spare the time to get up and go look for it, maybe you could lay your hands on a red-hot poker and put out both my eyes with it if this is what will make you feel better. Because you know what, Jerome? Your father just heard himself mention the subject of privacy, so he doesn't deserve whatever you decide in your mind is the very worst punishment?

Maybe you should call the FBI, Jerome.

So call the FBI because your father had the gall to talk to you from the bottom of his heart of hearts.

Do you hear me, Jerome? I am waiting for whatever punishment in your brilliant opinion would be the one I couldn't take. Because if just breathing your father makes such a loud noise you couldn't hear yourself think, all you got to do is pick up the telephone and tell them you want to report me for making a tumult it's a crime to make. So you'll call the G-men instead of the FBI if the FBI answers and they tell you right this minute they're so busy, darlings, they couldn't take the case.

Listen, Jerome darling, I want to give you every assurance your father would not blame you for one instant if you went and got another new unlisted on top of the one you just got. But why knock yourself out, darling? Use your common sense. You think your father would stand by and let you have to go all the way down to the telephone company and wait around to all hours until they get good and ready to inform you as to the ins and outs of your new digits? Believe me, cutie guy, you only have to ask and your father will spare you all this heartache. Because even if with just my mouth breathing, it's so loud you couldn't bear it in your brain, forget the phone company, all you got to do is speak up. Do you think I your father would deny you one shred of your happiness for one single instant? So why hesitate? A signal is all your father asks for. You wouldn't even have to lift a finger if the racket the blood in my veins makes happens to constitute such a terrible perturbance to your privacy you don't get the peace and quiet you need to be a genius. You could wink, darling. Lifting a finger, I definitely don't recommend it. Who knows, you might strain something—it's not worth it to take a chance. One wink, boychik, and all your worries will be over. One wink will be perfectly sufficient—believe me. Because your father will take it from there, your father will do all the running, whereas you yourself could just sit back and relax and forget it. Don't worry, you wouldn't even have to give me a whole wink if you decide in your mind you don't feel like it. Darling, you could give me maybe a mini-wink if this is your decision. Because I guarantee you, sweetheart, one mini-wink and already your father will be racing up the stairs of this building, hoping and praying in his heart of hearts the management didn't put no fence around the roof. So I apologize, Jerome, your father when he moved in didn't exhibit the foresight to go up and take a look in the first place.

But do I make myself clear, darling? Answer me, it is not going in one ear and out the other? Because I want you to know that your father could not kill himself fast enough if this is what it takes to make sure his sonny boy gets every last ounce of all the bliss he's got coming to him. But I ask you, pussycat, solitude? Are you telling me forever and forever solitude and seclusion is what it takes? Because your father is willing to learn, sweetheart, so tell me. So show me where it says solitude and seclusion is the same thing as happiness, and meanwhile one peep out of anybody who adores you to pieces is such a tragedy you definitely couldn't stand it. In black and white, Jerome, show me where this is written. Because as dumb as your father is, he is still keeping an open mind. But until you get ready to show me, in the interim don't excite yourself, darling, your father just gave you his solemn promise. If a telephone call or a post-card or a letter is such an agony for you that you couldn't take it, even if it's only for hello and good-bye and I hope I didn't disturb you, then relax, pussycat, don't worry, one mini-wink from you will settle the whole affair. Do you hear me? One mini-wink and your father will be only too happy and glad to make you a present of his own dead body. And you know what? You wouldn't even have to thank me for it if you're too busy being a genius and a hermit.

Are you listening to me, boychik? Are you paying strict attention? Your father is not talking just to hear himself talk? Because I can't rest for a single solitary instant until I make sure in my heart of hearts you heard me. Listen, maybe you should write it down as to the fact that your father is ready and willing to go to his grave in case his presence here on the earth doesn't give his boychik all the privacy he needs. Also, make a note that a full wink is utterly uncalled for. A little wiggle of the eyelid like you are maybe just thinking of winking but are probably too tired to do it, I promise you your father will run next door to another building if, God forbid, it turns out that this one here they put a fence on the roof. Sweetheart, I only hope and pray the upshot is I don't have to keep you waiting. As God is my judge, I'm sorry, but at my years and age, a fence, who knows, maybe I couldn't climb over it and meanwhile there's nobody up there who's waiting around to give me a boost. But even if the next building it's the same story, don't worry, darling, there's buildings up and down the block, and your father will just keep looking high and low until something works out.

This, sweetheart, is my solemn promise to you. And all I got to say is that I am down on my hands and knees thanking God that your father still got the strength in his body to give you his sworn statement in writing. But, believe me, Jerome, if it turns out that in all these years this is what you needed, you only had to say so. Because it's just like with the man who goes to get the suit. So he says to the tailor, "You'll make me a suit—whatever it costs, it costs, I want the best, so don't worry." And the tailor says to him, "Okay, I'm sparing nothing. The cloth I'm getting special from Borneo, the thread I'll have made up in China, and for the buttons I am thinking in terms of a yak they got in Turkey, buttons from the horns of that yak." So the man says to the tailor, "This sounds to me like a wonderful suit, so when can I get it?" and the tailor says to him, "A production like this, from here and from there, everything made up to order, we're talking six, eight months *minimum*." So the man says, "Six, eight months! How can I wait six, eight months if I got a bar mitzvah this Saturday and I was thinking of wearing the suit?"

Jerome darling, would you like to listen with your own two ears to what that tailor said to that man? Because this is what he said to him. He said, "You need it, you'll get it."

So do I make myself clear, Jerome? Why stand on ceremony? You'll wiggle your eyelid a little and in two seconds your father will take himself right out of the picture.


Meanwhile, who knows, maybe I am jumping to too many conclusions. Maybe 603 wasn't working right because of the High Holy Days, such a strain all of a sudden on the electricity. Let's face it, you got sons and daughters galore calling all day down here from all the different area codes, and meanwhile your father is the only person who is calling in the opposite direction, maybe I got some kind of funny hookup and it wasn't even 603 in the first place. But be this as it may, you still do not say go get lost to a person when he is asking you a perfectly civilized question. Listen, darling, please God they don't get fired up there in 603 and come down here to 305 looking. Because I am entirely at liberty to tell you that with a mouth on them like the one your father heard, they don't hire you so fast in this area code down here. Not even if you got in your pocket the personal recommendation of a genius!

Jerrychik sweetie, it's forgotten and forgiven, so let's forgive and forget it. Meanwhile, it's the High Holidays again, so is this the right time for bitterness and recrimination? Sweetie boy, it's water under the bridge. So let's do ourselves a favor and change the conversation. It's a fresh start, boychik. So what if it's another whole year down the crapper and everything is still under par at your end of the bargain? You think your father is keeping score with regard to the question of who sends who cards and letters, never mind who doesn't even place a simple phone call? So big deal if everybody else in 305 is getting. You think I don't know I don't have the right to expect a little decency and consideration when it could always happen you might get a rupture from lifting the wrong pencil? Listen, perish the thought that your father should even look twice at a mailman. Why kid ourselves? Who remembers what one of them even looks like anymore, it's been so many years since a person had the pleasure.

Listen, darling, before you forget, with your own two hands you better check around for the nearest blunt instrument. Because I hear myself talk to you and what is it I hear but criticism after criticism? Promise me, Jerome, you won't spend too much money. So long as it's good and heavy, go ahead and make the investment and then give it to me right between the eyes or on the back of my head, whichever you decide in your mind is more convenient. Because here I am, writing to bring you High Holiday greetings, and what am I bringing but recrimination after recrimination in spite of my honest intentions. And even if it's all for your own benefit, Jerome, I still say shame on me, shame on me! Look, when you get through with the blunt instrument, you should leave instructions for them to put your father in the gas chamber and keep him on bread and water. No leniency, Jerome—your father didn't earn in his lifetime one iota! The gas chamber and then the rubber hose, Jerome, even this is still too good for a person of my caliber.

Sonny boy, can you find it in your heart of hearts to wipe the slate clean? Because so far as your father is concerned, from this very instant it's a whole new ballgame. It's like we're starting from the outset, okay? Whatever I said, promise me, darling, you erased it. I mean, it just occurred to me you maybe sent a little something but you forgot about the zip code. A genius like you with so much on his brain, so who's got room in a thing like that for so many extra numbers? So ask yourself, you leave off the zip code, do the morons deliver? Believe me, you're just lucky if they don't also come after you to your own personal address and tear you limb from limb.

It's the truth, Jerrychik—nothing is these days what it used to be, not in any shape, manner, or form. It's not like it was in the old days. Tell me, darling, you remember how it was in the old days when you were at the top of the heap and your father was down here up in the penthouse? So guess who is in the penthouse now. Because the Allen people is the answer! And after them, it's the Krantzes which is second on the list to get in there. But in the good old days, it was all different. These days, maybe you got the right idea, a hermit. Believe me, don't think your father hasn't considered. I look at it the way it is these days and I have to say to myself, "Sol, maybe we should all go live where the operator hears they are looking for you and she tells them, whoever they are, beat it, forget it, take a walk, you dumb cluck."

These days, Jerome, it's things of every description, and just a fraction of it is enough to make your father vomit. Go look if you don't believe me. Like even in the kindergarten you hear the teacher say to the children it's milk time, take out your milk and drink it. But, lo and behold, nowadays there is always one child which wouldn't touch the milk. So the one I have in mind, his name is Arnold, and the teacher says to him, "Arnold, drink your milk." But how does Arnold answer this woman? You wouldn't believe this, Jerome, but he says to her, "I wouldn't drink the goddamn milk."

This, Jerome, is how in this day and age a child answers. So I don't have to tell you, the teacher goes right to the telephone and she calls the child's mother and she says to this woman to come over. So when the woman gets there, the teacher says to the mother, "I want you to hear this," and then she says to Arnold, "Arnold, drink your milk."

Jerome, as I live and breathe, this is how the child answers her back the second time. He says to her, "Not only I wouldn't drink the goddamn milk, but you could also shove it up your tookis."

Did you hear this, Jerome? Can you in all your born days believe it?

So you know what happens next? Darling, that teacher turns to that mother and she says to the woman, "Did you hear what your son just said?" Jerome, I am ashamed to say it, but that mother turns to that teacher and says to her, "Sure, I heard him—fuck him."

Sonny boy, this is what today's world is. And don't worry, boychik, your father noticed. But speaking of the subject of mothers, Jerome, I just remembered something. Because maybe you called to say hello and I wasn't here to answer. So even if you called at night, it could have happened, darling, your father not here to pick it up because of a certain Mrs. Pinkowitz, and I am not for one instant ashamed to admit it.

I know I don't need to remind you that your father is a grown man, Jerome. In case you didn't realize, your father is an adult. So as a grown man and as an adult, excuses I don't have to make to anyone, a certain resident of 603 included. Sonny boy, these are the facts of life, and it wasn't your father which invented them.

So now you know. So it was only one night, but now you know, so sue me, so call Clarence Darrow and sue me.


Listen, Jerrychik, between father and son, honesty is the best policy, this is my personal opinion. So it's speaking along these lines, darling, that it is time to come to the subject of Gert Pinkowitz. Do I make myself crystal clear, Jerome? Because even in my health and my years, I thank God that romance is not totally out of the picture. But first and foremost, Jerome, your father is the type of person who gives comfort where comfort is due. Now you take the creature previously referred to, for your information this is a person with enough heartache for an army. If you can believe it, darling, even worse than your father, this person suffers and suffers. Not in all your born days could you even guess! But who knows, maybe I already told you what a svelte and adorable creature Gert Pinkowitz is, not to mention that she is also an individual which could give your father cards and spades when it comes to the question of how much agony a human being could receive at the hands of their own flesh and blood. And guess what, boychik— just like your own personal father, it's a son which is the source as to where every last shred of Gert Pinkowitz's tragedy is coming from.

Tell me, sweetheart, did you ever think you would live to see the day when I your father would run smack into such a terrific coincidence? Listen, I know it's a small world, but a thing like this is definitely unbelievable—right here in this same building a creature just like your father which also got a son who you could break a blood vessel and die from.

But who knows if I already made mention? Maybe I did or maybe I didn't in a prior communication. On the other hand, darling, since I didn't write to you the day before yesterday, then I have to say to myself, "Face facts, Sol, you didn't." Because when you stop to consider the arithmetic, boychik, it's only twenty-four hours since the woman first set foot on the premises here and established her residence in this building.

So okay, sweetie darling, your father has been seeing a certain svelte person, it is nothing to be ashamed of. So what if it is a whirlwind romance? You think I can't see where the arithmetic speaks for itself? Meanwhile, it couldn't be avoided, two creatures which are both available and got so much unhappiness in mutual.

This is fate, boychik. This is what it means when you ask them for the whys and the wherefores and they say to you it's fate and you could stand on your left ear but you couldn't avoid it. Like with the fella who says to his brother, "So go to Miami and don't worry, I promise you I'll watch out for the cat, it'll be all right, in its whole life the cat wouldn't get better looking after." So the brother who's so crazy about his cat goes to Miami, Jerome, and when he gets there, the first thing he does is he picks up the telephone and he calls his brother which is still in New York and he says to him, "So how's the cat?"

Listen, Jerome. Because I want you to hear how the brother in New York answers the brother in Miami when he says to him, "The cat's dead."

So naturally it's a long silence with no one talking. And then the brother in Miami says, "You're some brother I got! I ask you how's the cat, and you answer me, bing bang, the cat's dead! What kind of a way is this to say a thing to a brother, bing bang, the cat's dead? Believe me, you should learn how to say a thing when a person asks you a question—not just bing bang, no preliminaries, no fanfares, the cat's dead! Next time somebody asks you, you say you took the cat up to the roof for a little breath of air and she got a sniffle and you got her in the bed and in a few days, please God, she'll be up and around as good as new. So then when I telephone back in a couple of hours to ask you what's what with the cat, you say to me, well, there's complications, you're getting in a specialist, but with God's help she will pull through—not no bing bang, no overtures, the cat's dead! So when I call again to check with you what the specialist said, this is when you say to me you never know, there's no guarantee, the cat you had to rush to the hospital two seconds ago and even with the top men in medical science, lo and behold, the cat passed away. This is how a brother speaks to a brother, not bing bang, the cat's dead!"

So the brother that's in New York, Jerome, he says to the brother in Miami, "Look, I'm sorry, next time I'll know better, I promise you." So this is when the brother who is in Miami says to the brother in New York, "Forget it. So it's only a cat. Meanwhile, more important, how's Mother?"

Jerome darling, are you listening to this? Did you hear when the brother in Miami says to him, "So meanwhile how is Mother?" Now pay attention, darling, because I want you to also hear what the brother in New York says to the brother in Miami, because this is what he says to him verbatim. He says, "Mother?" He says, "Well, I'll tell you, Mother I took up to the roof for a little breath of air."

This is fate, boychik—this is fate and there is no two ways about it. So between your father and Gert Pinkowitz it's the same story—it's fate whichever direction you look at it from. And don't kid yourself, two individuals in our situation, it couldn't be avoided even if you whistled Dixie.

Okay, so at this point, I admit it, everything is still in the dating stage. But even with Romeo, you had to have your dating stage before it got around to this, that, the other. Believe me, your father is a patient man, Jerome—thirty-six hours, forty-eight hours, for a living doll like this, a person so svelte, your father could make an exception and wait to count all his chickens.

But for some things, sweetheart, patience is already beside the point, patience wouldn't make the big difference.

Sonny boy, Jerome darling, do me a favor and listen to me—because your father is here to tell you that in certain departments not even the patience of a saint would do the trick, and that goes even for the patience of a Jack Benny.

So call the G-men, Jerome. And if the G-men wouldn't give you total satisfaction, then maybe you could get somewhere with the Supreme Court or the Food and Drug. Darling, just so long as you know your father couldn't help himself, he has to speak up. *Enough is more than enough!*

So first you will take your time and decide which one you want to call to come and get me. And in the meanwhile, your father gives you his promise, he wouldn't budge from this very spot. Also, I wouldn't even put up a fight when they get down here with their handcuffs.

Jerome, I am giving you every assurance, darling, your father will go quietly, he wouldn't even begin to make a fuss.

But if you are asking me to keep my mouth shut when

it comes to the question of the envelope, from the bottom of my heart of hearts, I am sorry, Jerome—but this I could not promise you, not even if they made a law.

Cutie fellow, pussycat, stop to ask yourself—your father gets to the end of this letter, what comes next? Because the answer is the envelope. So just like it was first the cat and then the mother, here is another one where it is a question of fate and you couldn't in all your life avoid it. Sonny boy, you leave off the zip code and they don't deliver. So ask yourself, how much leeway does your father get, could he leave off two-thirds of a person's whole name?

No, he couldn't. But also could your father write it any different from how he has been writing it all these many years and years?

Darling, this is a question you don't need your father to answer.

Just so you know in advance that I your father tried to give this question every last ounce of consideration. But meanwhile, Jerome, the answer is forget it with this J.D. thing—because even if they made a law, not on a bet could your father ever do it! You hear me, darling? Not even if the G-men took the case and came down here with all their badges. Not even if the Supreme Court said to me, "Sol, it went nine to nothing against you, so for life it's Leavenworth, forget it."

Jerrychik, your father is an old man. But whatever the future holds, he would spend every minute of it in chains before he would go along with you on what you did to the wonderful name you had.

Listen, kiddo, you could go to Woolworth's and you could buy thumbtacks. Darling, you could even buy carpet tacks if this is your particular preference. So go ahead and buy whichever variety that pleases you and come stick them in my elbows. Okay, so if the elbows don't interest you, I'll give you a choice, you can choose the kneecaps instead. So choose the kneecaps, Jerome. Believe me, if this is what you decide in your mind, then this is what you decide in your mind—kneecaps, your father wouldn't for two seconds stand in your way even if you begged him. Tell me, boychik, are you getting the picture? Because the picture is this, Jerome—in every last department your father is only too happy and glad to go along with you, but this J.D. thing you did to your name, this he could never get used to! This thing here is where he has to draw the line!

I'm sorry, sweetheart, but J.D. I couldn't go along with, not even if they came down here with their handcuffs and shot me down like a dog. Because by me, darling, the name you were born with, you could go ahead and ask anyone, they'll tell you it is a symphony of music to the most discriminating of ears.

I promise you, sonny boy, you could go to the ends of the earth and you still couldn't improve on it. Just to listen to it! So are you listening?

*Jerome David.*

Now tell me that's not the last word when it comes to a gorgeous symphony of names.

But a thing like J.D., Jerome, since when is a thing like J.D. a name?

Cutie guy, you want to kill your father with this thing of J.D., then go ahead and kill me with it. But meanwhile don't ask me to write it on the envelope. Because if this is what you are asking, darling, then you are asking for what your father will not give!


Stop to think, pussycat. Promise me you won't excite yourself and you will stop to think for all of two seconds.

So first of all, answer me the following question. There isn't a thoroughfare called Jerome in the Bronx? As thoroughfares go, it's not one which down through the ages is a thoroughfare that is famous and respected?

So is this a simple question? And does a person have to be a genius to give it a simple answer?

Sonny boy, take my word for it, when the city fathers sat down to pick a name, they didn't say to themselves, "So let's pick a shtunky one for this one here."

Okay, I admit it, so maybe it was the borough fathers which sat down. It's still the same principle. Believe me, darling, right here in the Sunshine State, where I your father bring you High Holy Day greetings from, on Lincoln Avenue they got a Jerome Florists. On Lincoln Avenue, darling. So am I talking about a first-class thoroughfare? Look for yourself, as big as life, a Jerome Florists. And it's not just here or there, darling—because it's *Lincoln* Avenue, not to mention it's also a corner location!

But listen, a father does not know a son? I need all of a sudden a mind-reader to tell me what's in my sonny boy's head? So arrest me because I happen to know my own child. Tell them to come and lock up your father on bread and water in Death Row because I happen to be an expert on the question of my sonny boy's brain. Meanwhile, you can stand on your left ear but you cannot change the rule that says it takes a father to know a son. Jerome, they could come and cut off both my arms. They could chop me up in little pieces. But I your father am here to tell you, a father knows a son.

Guess what, darling. Are you listening to me, Jerome? To the fathers of this world, a son is what is eating your heart out—and I and the other fathers don't need no Walter Winchell to come along and give us this particular news.

But don't think I don't know I should learn to keep my

125

mouth shut. Believe me, Jerome, they should come and cut your father's throat from ear to ear until he learns to bite his tongue. Lincoln Avenue—I had to go ahead and say Lincoln Avenue. So does a father have to go to college to find out what is in his sonny boy's head? Don't kid yourself, Jerome, your father can hear every last word you are thinking. Does a father know a son? I guarantee you, darling, your father could quote you your exact phraseology, word for bitter word.

"So how come they didn't name me Lincoln?"

Boychik, tell me the truth, was that verbatim? Open your heart of hearts to me and tell me, did your father just quote you every last word?

Don't tell me the answer because I know the answer. And you know why, Jerome? Because a father knows a son! And you know what else, darling? The more brilliant the brain of the child, the more you cannot please him—not even if you did a dance and stood on your left ear.

Kiddo, this is what your father knows. You could talk yourself blue in the face, but this is what your father knows.

Oh, but you really got a lot to complain about, Jerome— a father which gave you such a gorgeous name and then has the gall to write it down on an envelope instead of something it makes him heartsick to even mention out loud. Believe me, I never saw a boy with more to complain about. But don't kid yourself, sonny, it's no picnic for me neither. I promise you, all I need is an excuse and I'll show you it's a subject your father couldn't drop fast enough. But so long as you didn't give me an excuse yet, it couldn't hurt to mention a few comparisons.

Like take, for instance, a certain Mrs. Roth who lives in this building. So tell me, darling, does she have a relation who is a Philip or a P.? Or look instead at the Bellow people who got such a nice oceanview on 10. Ask yourself, do they have a second cousin named Saul or a second cousin named

S.? The Malamuds on 6, a one-bedroom facing front, we're talking in this case about a Bernard in the family or a B.?

Please God, darling, you stopped and took a good look at these questions, and then you answered each and every one of them from deep down in your heart of hearts.

But now we come to your father, Jerome. Do you appreciate what I am saying to you, Jerome—now we come to your own flesh and blood? Who is *also* a resident of this building! Who is *also* a person who has to live with these people! Who is *also* a person who has to answer to them! And what, pray tell, is the question?

Jerome, the question is, "J.D., Mr. Ess—what, please be so kind, is a J.D.?"

Cutie guy, pay attention—down here in 305 a Saul they heard of, a Philip, a Bernard. But since when did somebody in 305 ever hear of a J.D.? Stop to think, boychik. Because in this building this is the question your father has to answer to morning, noon, and night. And you know for how many years now? Day in and day out, you know for how many?

This is why I say to you, Jerome, thank God for Gert Pinkowitz. This is why I have to say to you thank God for the heartache she's got with her own kid, because for your father it's a lesson to see there's those that got worse—even if I wouldn't wish it on my own worst enemy.

Twenty-four hours, Jerome, the woman is in the building only twenty-four hours, and already the gang of them found better to talk about! So for how many years was it your father? And *now* what? Jerome, I'll tell you. Now it's Gert Pinkowitz!

But believe me, I don't wish the woman ill. For Gert Pinkowitz, your father has got nothing but hearts and flowers. It's just I couldn't take it no more—J.D. this and J.D.

that, years and years, day in and day out, the whole building couldn't leave you for one instant in peace. Besides, darling, svelte as Gert is, the woman is made of iron. Of *iron.*

Listen, Jerome, forget Gert Pinkowitz for all of two seconds. Because your father requires your utmost attention. Cutie fellow, will you give me your very utmost? Because it is time for your father to go down on his hands and knees to you again and beg you to please in your heart of hearts reconsider.

Jerome, listen to me, where does your father live, which building?

Since years and years ago when he moved down here, has he ever for one instant lived in a different residential?

All right, so what would you call this place—a building like any other building?

Jerome, don't make me have to remind you.

Sweetheart, we are talking the Seavue Spa Oceanfront Garden Arms and Apartments. So do you need reminding which is your father's residential? Because for how many years now have I been telling you? But do you ever listen?

Other children listen, Jerome. The Allen kid, Woody, *he* listens. *Philip* listens, *Saul* listens—and for your information, so does *Bernard!* Believe me, Jerome, everybody in here, they got a kid which they can count on to listen—the Krantzes do and the Plains do, and so do the Sheldons and the Friedmans and the Elkins and the Wallaces and the Segals and the Jaffes and the Barretts and the Bernsteins and the Halberstams! And notice that I am not even mentioning the Robbins family and their Harold, and the Potoks and their Chaim. You think the Wouks don't have a Herman which listens?

The Mailer people, their Norman *listens.*

You heard of the Brodkeys, the Adlers? So tell me, the one's got a boy and the other's got a girl which don't listen?

The Kordas got a Michael, and *he* listens!

The Apples with their Max, the Michaels people with their Leonard, the Stones with their Irving—every last one of these children is a child which listens! And did I even get to the Markfields and the Richlers and the Liebowitzes? Ozick, you think this is a girl which doesn't listen? So answer me—is she a Cynthia or a C.? The Charyns, you heard of the Charyns? So they also got a child which listens—and, pay attention, his name is *Jerome* and not no *J.*, into the bargain!

Sweetheart, I didn't even begin to scratch the surface yet of who's who in the Seavue Spa Oceanfront Garden Arms and Apartments! But answer me, is there a single solitary one of them which doesn't have a relation in the literature business? And exclusive of the exception of your father and Mrs. Pinkowitz, tell me if it is not a kid which doesn't take to heart what you say to him and *listens!*

In the whole building, they all got what to listen to them—all except your father and Gert Pinkowitz, all except her with her Thomas and me with my J.D., the two big geniuses which wouldn't for one minute listen!

And look at who I didn't even discuss yet—not to mention the Millers and the Hellers and the Ephrons and the Kosinskis! Do the Paleys have a Grace? So tell me, Jerome, the Sontags don't got a Susan? Is either the one or the other a girl which does not listen?

The Olsens got a Tillie, and the Golds got a Herbert, and the Uris family, they got there a wonderful, sweet-natured boy, a Leon—but what else do they have which your own personal father doesn't have?

I will answer you in words of one syllable, Jerome. Because the answer is *a child which listens!*

Jerome, darling, your father is hoarse from screaming. Even though your father is writing and not talking, Jerome—I

promise you, your father just lost his voice from the screaming. So call the Justice Department, your father had to shout.
Because to make himself heard with you, who could talk
like a civilized person?

Darling, sonny darling, lean close, open your ears up
wide, I couldn't speak no more above a whisper.

So who is in the penthouse here when it used to be
your father who was up there? And you know the answer
why?

Because they got a child which listens! And you know
what, Jerome? The boy's name is not no W. Allen neither!

But far be it from me your father to pass comment.
After all, your father is only your father, Jerome. He is only
the person which has to live here with these people and
answer to them. He is only the person which has to face
these people day in and day out because in his particular
area code you don't get away with saying to the whole wide
world, "Do me a favor and go take a walk."

Jerrychik, sweetie boy, is it asking too much for you
to look into your heart of hearts and try to see what is going
on down here from your father's side of the standpoint? Do
I live in the Seavue Spa Oceanfront Garden Arms and Apartments or do I live in the woods in a tree? And as to this
residential, Jerome, we're talking from one floor to the next
what? Are we talking people which got kids in cloaks and
suits, or are we talking people which got kids in books?

The works, Jerome—the cream of the crop of the literature business is right here in this very building, and I
want to remind you that it is your father, and not you, which
is the person that has to live with them!

But did you ever stop to think, "For my father, considering that he is a person of his age and his years, I, Jerome
David, am going to ask myself what is it like to live in a
setup where everybody's got somebody in the business"?

Darling, your father will put two and two together for you and answer you with one word. So do you want to hear what the one word is?

C-O-M-P-A-R-I-S-O-N-S.

*Comparisons*, Jerome. Notice, like *privacy*, your father can also spell this one too. And, believe me, it comes out the opposite of GET LOST.

So you are not a genius in your own right and I got to draw for you a diagram? You need me to write down for you Saul this and Saul that, Phillie this and Phillie that— not to mention Woody, Woody, Woody until your father's got it coming out of both ears?

You could live to be a thousand, Jerome, you still wouldn't see any letup. But meanwhile does your father ever get to get a word in? Does he hear Jerome this and Jerome that the way he used to hear in the old days when guess who lived in the penthouse? But God forbid the facts of life should be brought to your attention. So stick a spear in me and break it off in my ribs because your father has the nerve to plead with you for your attention when it is the facts of life which is the subject that's on the table. Boychik, you know what it means where it says the facts of life? It means somebody has to live with them! So just for argument's sake, darling, between the two of us, guess which one got elected!

Listen, in 603, let's not kid ourselves, so it's no big deal to walk around with two initials. Even with three or four, maybe up there in your area code they still wouldn't look at you cross-eyed. But in 305, Jerome, I hope I don't have to tell you, they find out you got a kid who calls himself J.D., you couldn't live long enough, you'll never hear the end of it. Meanwhile, who's complaining? Believe me, I know I got plenty to be grateful for. Because when you hear what Gert Pinkowitz has got with *her* brilliant genius, you'll see why your father is only too happy and glad to sit down and count every last one of his blessings.

But you'll promise me, boychik, you'll reconsider? Because this is all your father asks of you, two whole seconds of heartfelt reconsideration. Darling, I am down on my hands and knees to you asking. God forbid in all my life I should ever ask again. Please, darling, if you hear me even thinking to ask, you'll run out and get railroad spikes and hammer them into my shins. But meanwhile, for all of two seconds, Jerome, I am begging you to sit down with yourself and like a civilized person you will go into conference with your heart of hearts and you will say to yourself, "For my father's sake, who would let me hammer even rusty railroad spikes into his shins for me, I, Jerome David, am going to think this question over and change my spiteful ways."

Cutie sonny, what your father is asking you can ask anybody and they will tell you it is not too much to ask. Look, you'll let your better judgment be your guide—and whatever you decide in your mind, just remember that your father knows you will be a good boy and come to your senses and decide the right thing. And if I ever utter one more word in this particular department, may I inherit the whole Waldorf-Astoria and drop dead in every single room.


By the bye, sweetheart, you'll never guess what the Roth woman said to me last week. Because when she said it to me, right away your father said to himself, "I can't wait to tell the sonny boy what this woman is saying to me, please God he will go along with his father's thinking and realize that you never know where wisdom is going to come from next." So here is the quote, Jerrychik. You'll listen closely and you'll tell me what you think of this quotation. She said, "Mr. Ess, tell me, did you ever stop to realize that when he

stood up and had to swear on a stack of Bibles, they said to
him, 'Do you, Dwight David Eisenhower,' and so on and so
forth? But pay attention, they didn't say to the man no D.D."
Darling, you can't argue with what the woman said.
Believe me, I myself stood there and said to myself, "You
know, Sol, this woman is speaking the truth—it's right there
in the history books in black and white."
Believe me, Jerome, this is wisdom. So whatever the
source, I say you've got to hand it to the woman, she spoke
wisdom pure and simple, and you don't go look a gift horse
in the mouth. But if you couldn't bear to hear it, Jerome, if
even history isn't good enough for you, then tell them to
come down here and take my shoes off and make your father
jump up and down on broken glass. All right, I grant you,
you didn't decide yet in your own mind that you want them
to swear you in as the President of the United States. This
your father grants you, this much your father acknowledges.
But the principle is still the same thing, Jerome—don't kid
yourself, in every way, shape, manner, and form what you
have is still the same principle.
Cutie fellow, sweetie fellow, boychikeleh mine, go back
to the gorgeous name your father gave you and you wouldn't
have to hold your breath for the world to be your oyster all
over again. This is my written guarantee to you, Jerome.
Get rid of this J.D. thing, and I promise you, you'll feel like
a brand-new person. And don't think that in two seconds
everybody won't notice. Before you know it, they'll all be
singing your praises just the way they used to, the whole
gang of them in the literature industry, not to mention their
families and relations. Believe me, darling, they'll all be
saying to themselves, "God love him, he's some terrific kid,
that kid, look how after all these years he did the right thing
and made his father happy."
Pay attention, boychik, they are definitely not no dum-
mies, these kids that also went with you into the literature

business. And even if there's plenty of them your father looks at and has to say to himself, "That one there, to tell you the truth, I don't see what they see in him," even the worst of them your father can tell you they still got a head on their shoulders and are only too willing to take off their hat to a person which does the right thing when it is a question of his father's wishes. Are you listening to me, sweetheart? They'll hear what you did, and even the Allen kid will step aside and tell you to go back up to the top of the heap. All it takes is for you to show them you made up your mind to be a serious person with a serious name that makes sense to decent people.

Your father is speaking to you without favoritism, Jerome. Your father is speaking to you the way a Solomon would speak to you if the man was alive to tell you himself. Your father does not play favorites, Jerome. Believe me, your father does not give you one shred of credit you don't deserve. So when he tells you all you got to do is go back to being Jerome David again, your father is giving you his absolutely honest appraisal. Darling, please give me some credit for intelligence! Your father doesn't give a person his honest appraisal until he's weighed every one of the whys and wherefores. Phillie, Saul, Bernie, and the rest of them, they'll hear what you did and they wouldn't be able to get out of your way fast enough. Are you listening, Jerome? Because I am taking into consideration not just exclusively these youngsters and the Allen kid but also your other top people in this building, which if you look up on 16 just under the penthouse, you're talking the Robbins family and the Krantz family and the Sheldons. But meanwhile ask yourself, darling, in the case of the aforementioned, is it S. or is it Sidney? Is it J. or is it Judith? And Harold, you could ask anybody, it's Harold!

You see what your father is saying to you, boychik? So do me a favor and don't make me repeat myself. Tomorrow morning, first thing, it's a clean slate, okay? Believe me, your father can hear them already, it's such a shout in my heart, it's such music in my ears. "Say hello, everybody, to Solly's terrific cutie guy, Jerome David, a thoroughly new person!"

And another thing, darling—don't kid yourself, the King of Sweden is no dumbbell neither. Ask anyone. You ask anyone, Jerrychik, they'll be only too happy and glad to tell you the King of Sweden didn't just get off the boat. Go ahead, ask anyone, and they'll tell you the man is paying very close attention to who writes down his name on his book like there is something in it he is proud of and who puts down a name like the whole deal from start to finish was just a lick and a promise. Believe me, the King of Sweden comes along and sees a thing like just J.D., you think the man can't draw his own conclusions? Cutie guy, you could cut out my tongue for telling you—but your father didn't have to go to no college to know the King of Sweden has got eyes in his head, the man could add up two and two. So the man sees where it says you didn't have the heart to put your whole name down, just don't be surprised, Jerome, when he says to himself, "This one here, he's not fooling no King of Sweden nohow!"

But don't look at *me*, Jerome. I promise you, the King of Sweden can see for himself. I told you, I your father did not make the rules, not even the ones you didn't think up yourself.


So tell me, sweetheart, the plots I sent you last time, did any of them work out for you or was I wasting my breath? So if in your opinion nothing looked good to you, don't worry, I already got a couple a dozen new ones from keeping my eyes and ears wide open in the card room. Listen, in just my regular Wednesday game there's Charlie Heller, Mort

Segal, and Artie Elkin, and between the four of us, believe me, we could fill a whole library from top to bottom. By the bye, darling, I want you to guess what Mortie said to your father only two days ago. Because as God is my witness, Jerome, the man said to me, "Sol, do the child a favor and tell him to get rid of it. My Eric, for instance, he *added*, he didn't take away. So the boy wants a little flourish, a little trim, he *adds* a letter and gets Erich, whereas he meanwhile doesn't let three perfectly good letters go altogether to waste." So Mortie says, "Go tell your kid he could add a thing maybe, like a little trim thing over an E, whereas David he could make Davidorf—it's up to him. But the principle is you *add*, Sol, you don't take away."

Sonny, to tell you the truth, your father in his own mind never thought of this before. So for what it's worth, boychik, I your father am passing along to you a mere possibility, you don't have to hurry up and make a decision. But to your father's way of thinking, the name Jerome with a little trim on the top of it is definitely not the worst idea in the whole wide world. So who knows, the King of Sweden might even get a kick out of it. Because if you ask me, the man must have looked at the name Saul and he said to himself, "This here is a name which looks a little skimpy to me, a little fixing up here and there couldn't hurt it. But meanwhile I don't have to put up with just an S. Meanwhile you can see this Saul has got his heart in the right place."

Darling, the upshot of this I don't have to remind you. A medal! Thousands and thousands of dollars and a medal!

Be smart, Jerome. Listen to what Mort Segal says. You *add*, you don't take *away*. Believe me, maybe the man's got nothing but an Erich, but he knows as to whereof he speaks.

Which reminds me, sweetie boy—before I get to the subject of your father and his new excitement in life, it just this instant dawned on me to tell you that I noticed it's another year but what's what with you and Merv Griffin? Cutie fellow, if I have said it to you once, I have said it to you a million times, no business and no pictures is bad enough—but no Merv Griffin you definitely got to realize you can't get away with!

You know what you are, Jerome?

Because the answer is you are your own worst enemy!

All right, no pictures is a fact of life your father is learning to live with. So forget pictures. You don't want to have a picture, then don't have a picture. So maybe a genius doesn't have to have a picture. Only a handful of days ago I said to Murray Mailer, I said, "Murray, believe me, when you are a genius in your own right, then you will know you don't need a picture." I said to the man, "Listen, Murray, I myself am not questioning if your Norman is a genius. I am just saying if you are one, then you know you could live without pictures."

Jerome, I wouldn't even begin to tell you what the man said to me. But at the Seavue, do they ever give you the least little consideration? Jerome, the man stands there and he says to me, "Sol, this fella Einstein, like with the hair and the sweater and the pop-eyes? The man wasn't a genius? So tell me, Sol, how come you know what I'm talking about? You met him? You sat down to a meal with the man and broke bread with him? You saw a *picture*—wherever you looked, you saw a *picture*. But pardon me, my friend, I forgot—your kid with the initials is a bigger genius."

So please God Murray Mailer should live and be well, Jerome, but from him, I guarantee you, your father does not need a lesson in history. Meanwhile, I say you cannot discount the man totally. Believe me, darling, in this world, whatever the source, a person tells you something you never heard before, then you got to sit down and think it over and give that person credit. So it's the truth, darling, and in my own mind I never stopped to think about it before. But am I ashamed to admit it? So all right, Einstein was a big genius, the biggest—but even him, the biggest genius, he had a picture here, a picture there, pictures, pictures, pictures.

Believe me, sonny boy, I as your father am not holding Murray Mailer up to you. But let's face the music—the man knows wherefrom he speaks.

Sweetheart, I want to speak to you as your own father, an individual who does not play favorites. Jerome, you know what? You got on you a face like an angel! Do you hear me, Jerome? An angel!

But if a picture is for you such a trial and tribulation, then I say forget it, darling, you don't have to knock yourself out for no Murray Mailer's benefit, not to mention for the millions and millions of fans who would get down on their hands and knees to you to thank you for one single solitary exception if you only had it in your heart of hearts to make it.


Believe me, Jerome, I am washing my hands of the whole subject. You don't want a picture? Then don't have a picture! On the one hand no picture, and on the other hand a name like J.D. when that's not a name which makes any sense to anybody down here, these are things that are killing your father, but he never said he couldn't learn to live with them. Whereas the question of no Merv Griffin, Jerome, *this*, for your information, is a whole different question altogether!

Jerome darling, answer me this. Do I have to tell you what goes on down here when it's four o'clock in the afternoon at the Seavue Spa Oceanfront Garden Arms and Apartments? Answer me, Jerome, I didn't tell you enough times already?

Jerome, it is four o'clock, and where is everybody suddenly running? From the card room and from the pool and from everywhere in sight, where are all these hotshots in such a hurry to get to?

Because the answer, Jerome, is Merv Griffin!

You don't believe me, go take a look in their apartments. You could look for yourself if you wouldn't take your father's own word for it. Four o'clock, where are they? They're looking to see who's the lucky family who's got a child on with Merv today and who are the morons which doesn't!

So stop to think, Jerome—did your father ever once have the pleasure?

But far be it from me to utter one word when it comes to your own father's peace of mind and happiness. Believe me, Jerome, first and foremost, your father is not an individual who asks for himself. So think, Jerome—if not for myself, then for who am I asking for?

Darling, please, do me a favor—go into conference with your heart of hearts and ask yourself how you could ask your father such a question when you already know the answer. I promise you, when you know, you know, and you do not require a father to sit down with you and draw you a diagram. Like the woman who hears the telephone and she goes to pick it up. Did I tell you about this, Jerome? This woman, she goes to pick it up and she says, "Hello?" Just like any normal, civilized person, Jerome, the woman says, "Hello?"

So there's a man there on the other end, Jerome, and I want you to hear what this man says to this woman—because, as God is my judge, he says to her, "I know what your name is and I know where you live and I know you can't wait for me to come over there and tear off every stitch you got on you and throw you down on the floor and do to you every filthy dirty thing I can think of."

You heard this man, Jerome? You heard what this man said to this woman? But now I want you to hear how this woman answers him. Because this is what she says to him, darling—she says, "So you know all this from just hello?"

Jerome, did you hear every word that woman said to that man?

So do me a favor, darling, and don't ask your father any questions when the answer is something you already in your own mind know.


Sweetheart, I am going to give you some quotes that will interest you—word-for-word verbatim.

Gus Krantz: "So, Mr. Ess, you tell me your little one is too *sen*sitive for Merv Griffin, he couldn't go on there and make a little in*tell*igent conver*sat*ion? Tsk, tsk, Mr. Ess, we all under*stand*, believe me. When a child is too *sen*sitive, who is it it's always a *tra*gedy for? Be*lieve* me, Mr. Ess, my heart goes out to you, because for the father it's *real*ly a tragedy. A mother, she could maybe *live* with it, but a *fa*ther?"

Burt Bellow: "With my own eyes I noticed, Mr. Ess, maybe J.D. stands for a girl and she wants to keep it a secret? Listen, you'll tell your daughter to talk to Merv, the man will figure out an angle. Meanwhile, God love her, ask her if she heard about my Saul, a medal and thousands and thousands of dollars."

Cutie guy, don't excite yourself. So there are worse quotes than the ones I just told you. But does your father even listen? I promise you, whatever it is, it goes in one ear and out the other.

Who listens to these people with their Merv Griffins and their Merv Griffins!

But meanwhile it is the principle of the thing which

to I as your father is interesting. And, Jerome, in case you didn't already figure it out for yourself, the principle is it is either Merv Griffin or you could go ahead and forget it!

Granted, for years in memoriam I tried to shield you with my own body. Granted, what your father has had to go through for you a million fathers couldn't do it. And I also grant you it's still not half of what Gert has got with her high and mighty Thomas. But, Jerome, darling, be a nice boy and make an exception. So what's the big production? You'll pick up the telephone and you'll call the man and you'll say to Merv you thought it over in your mind and you are ready to make an appearance.

Boychik, would your father begin to ask you if he saw even the slightest alternative? So tell them to strap me down and turn on the electricity, your father is asking for your own benefit!

Sonny sweetie, they could go ahead and give me all the volts they got, but your father still wouldn't hesitate to tell you all it takes is a little intelligence even when a person is a genius. But does this mean that to his dying day you haven't got your father's vote? Jerrychik darling, your father will go right down the line with you to his last breath regardless. Meanwhile, ask yourself, is it fair that you who are the child should never meet your father halfway—when he is your father and your elder and would die for you if this is what you demanded? So answer me, for your own father you couldn't sit down with Merv for all of two seconds and make a little civilized conversation? Bing bang and it's over and done with, you can pick yourself up and go back to your 603 and meanwhile your father in his mind could go to his grave in peace and quiet and contentment. Because I want to ask you a question, Jerome. Tell me, so how do you propose your father is supposed to answer these people year in and year out when they come down the next day to the card room and they say to me, "Tsk, tsk, Mr. Ess, we watched and watched, but we didn't see no J.D. sitting there with Merv Griffin"?

You want another quote, Jerome? I tried to protect you with my own body, darling, but you want another one?

Okay, here is one from Artie Elkin.

"Tell me the truth, Solly, it was a cut-rate nose-job and the girl couldn't ever again show her face again in public? Listen, my Stanley is very close to certain very big doctors. You want me to give him a call and see what maybe could be worked out for her if you know the right people?"

Jerrychik, this is what your father has to live with, quotes like this morning, noon, and night. Whereas one word from you, and it's a whole new ballgame. Pay attention, Jerome—you'll call up and say, "Merv, look, I haven't got all day—the answer is yes, so send a ticket and when do you want me?"

So you'll tell them to kill me and bury me alive under boulders, Jerome, but first you'll do this for your father. Because I am here to tell you, boychik, maybe Gert Pinkowitz is made of iron, but as to your father, he definitely isn't.

So the Everest Mountain should fall over on me for remarking, but when they put your father together, darling, they made a mistake and they just used flesh and blood.

Do you hear me, Jerome? I couldn't take it anymore, every weekday all my life no Merv Griffin and meanwhile your father keeps watching and waiting, please God his sonny boy will get some sense in his head and someday see the light!

You want me to quote you Artie Elkin again? Because what the man said to me only this morning you wouldn't believe it unless you heard it for yourself—so I want you to hear this, Jerome, because, believe me, you'll appreciate. Are you listening? The man said to me, "Sol, as to your J.D., did I or did I miss her? Four-thirty, four-forty, was she on there or wasn't she? Because maybe I left the room at the inopportune point of departure when I had to go see a man about a dog in the toilet. So was she or wasn't she? Even with the nose, did the girl take her chances? So tell me, Sol, what is the terrible verdict?"

Pussycat, what will it cost you to pick up the phone and tell Merv you are going to make an exception? As your father, am I or am I not entitled to a civilized answer?

Enough privacy for two seconds, Jerome! It wouldn't kill you! It is only Merv Griffin!

Jerome, I have to whisper again, I'm so hoarse from all this screaming. Darling, pay attention, we are talking about a wholesome show for the entire American family. So did you hear me? Please, you'll sit down with the man, you'll say hello and good-bye and take a look at my face—and then you'll get up and walk away on your own two feet, and I promise you, you'll thank me for every minute of it, and so will all of your fans from coast to coast overseas in every single direction.

Okay, so you don't have to give your father your answer this very instant.

You need to think it over in your mind, then go ahead and think it over in your mind. So in the morning your decision will be your decision, and you'll call Merv and advise the man accordingly. And don't forget to tell him to send you a round-trip ticket.

You know what, Jerome? Tonight, after I finish this letter, when your father finally puts his head on the pillow and says his prayers, I am going to thank God that with regard to the simple question of Merv Griffin my sonny boy and I have had a meeting of the minds and the subject is from start to finish all settled. And I promise you, I wouldn't even say boo to Artie Elkin and the rest of them beforehand. The gang of them should only be looking and not be ready for it when guess who walks out and Merv says, "Ladies and gentlemen, have I got for you the cream of the crop of the literature business!"

Jerome, I'll tell you something which just between you and your father will be our little secret. Artie and the rest of them, who wishes these gangsters ill? But when a certain person walks out and sits himself down to converse with Merv, every hoodlum in this building will drop dead! From one floor to the next, right up to the penthouse, all the bigshots will grab their kishkas and keel over. And you know what? Your father wouldn't blame them for one minute.

So call the Chinese Army and tell them to come and stick knitting needles under your father's fingernails, but this is what I am telling you. Even up in the penthouse with their Woody, they'll have to get the undertaker!

So the plots, Jerome, tell me, did you see anything there? Because since you're going to be going on Merv, it couldn't hurt to ask the man what he thinks of this here plot as against that one. Believe me, Jerome, the man knows. The man didn't just get off the boat, darling. Pay attention to your father—you ask Merv an intelligent question, the man will be only too happy and glad to give you the benefit of his wisdom.

The man knows the business, Jerome. Are you listening to me? Believe me, the man didn't get where he is from giving people bad advice. Listen, Jerrychik, you open your heart of hearts to Merv and, I promise you, you won't be sorry. The man knows whereof he speaks. Besides, does it ever hurt to ask? You'll show him the plots I sent you and then you'll sit down with him and you'll listen to him and you'll see what the man thinks. And meanwhile whichever ones he says to you, "Jerome David, these are the ones I want you to get rid of," don't forget to send them back to me, and your father will be a sport and make a present of them to Gert Pinkowitz.

Who knows, maybe God will make a miracle and the woman could get somewhere with one of them with her own kid.

Sweetheart, I didn't tell you yet what the story is in that department, did I? Believe me, I know you got a lot on your mind. Just getting ready to go back to your old name and be on Merv, I realize that this is plenty for the current agenda. But meanwhile, Jerome, when someone comes along who is suffering worse than you are, then you should always sit yourself down with that person and listen to their story— because I will tell you something, dearheart, you never know what you could learn from the trials and tribulations of the other person. Like the furrier who calls up his travel agent and he says to him, "Look, I'm sick to death of the usuals, give me what you got in the way of the Joneses couldn't keep up with it if it killed them," and the travel agent says to him, "Well, what do you say to a couple of weeks on a slave ship?" So the man says, "A slave ship? What's a slave ship?"

Jerome, the travel agent answers him like this—he says to the man, "A slave ship, a galley ship—you never heard of a galley ship?" And the man says, "Sure, I heard of a galley ship. Next time you're talking a galley ship, *say* a galley ship. So tell me, this season the right people are cruising on a galley ship? Then hurry up and book me a galley ship, first-class."

So the next thing you know, Jerome, it's time to go get aboard, and the man and his wife of forty years, they go down there, and they get on board, and it is absolutely gorgeous.

Darling, your father is here to tell you, this was some gorgeous ship this man and his wife got on. Service like this you never saw in your life. Hand and foot, they couldn't wait on you fast enough. So the man and his wife, they're in there in their stateroom and it's so gorgeous they can't believe it—when meanwhile here comes this terrible knocking on the door. And who is it, Jerome? Because I am here to tell you, it's this individual maybe seven feet tall, and he says to the man, "You Goldbaum?" So Goldbaum looks at him, seven feet tall, naked all over, these muscles, Jerome, such muscles. So Goldbaum looks and he winks and he says, "I'm Goldbaum."

Well, darling, this big naked man says to Goldbaum, "If you're Goldbaum, then it says here it's your turn at the oars." Do you hear this, Jerome, the *oars*? And the fellow is looking at this list he's got and he says, "Nathan Goldbaum, right?" So Goldbaum says to the man, "Oars?"

Jerome, this is when the big naked man gives Goldbaum a grab and pulls him out into the hall and he says to Goldbaum, "Fucking right, oars!"

Jerome, would you believe this? In all your born days, would you believe with your own ears what is happening here? Because they take Goldbaum down there into the bottom of the ship and they tear off the clothes he's got on his back and then they put these chains on his legs and they make him sit down and with all the other men he's got to pull on these oars until the ship is rowed all the way out of New York Harbor! But this is nothing, Jerome, nothing! Because meanwhile there's all these big fellows walking around and they're hitting Goldbaum and the rest of them such smacks. With whips!

*Whips*, Jerome!

Well, I don't have to tell you, it takes maybe two, three days to row out there—and in all this time, darling, did Goldbaum get one drink of water? Forget water! Not even a piece of *fruit*, Jerome. Hitting with whips, *this* is what Goldbaum and the rest of them got!

Meanwhile, okay, they get the ship rowed out there and the big fellow comes over and he gets the chains off Goldbaum and he has to pick him up and carry the man, this is the condition which Goldbaum is in!

But listen, darling, even in this condition, like a dead man, I want you to ask yourself what Goldbaum is thinking to himself when the big fellow is carrying him back to his stateroom like a rag which is no good for nothing.

Jerome darling, do you want me to answer you?

The man is *starved*, Jerome, the man is dying of *thirst*! And *bleeding*! Believe me, I don't have to describe to you the blood, it would make you sick if I told you just the half of it, how much blood Goldbaum already bled all over himself.

But meanwhile, Jerome, what is Goldbaum *thinking*?

Jerome darling, I want you to hear this. Because even in his condition, God love him, Goldbaum is thinking to himself, "So what do you tip a fella like this?"

Did you hear this, Jerrychik? "What do you tip a fella like this?" Did you hear every word of what Goldbaum is thinking to himself on the slave ship?

So this is why I say to you, darling, it never hurts to listen to the other person's pain and suffering. Believe me, Jerome, whatever the source, you could always learn something when you pay attention to the other fellow's aggravation. Even from Merv Griffin, you could learn, for instance. Because don't think the man hasn't been through plenty in his own right.

But on this earth, darling, even taking into account

your own personal father, there is *nobody* what got the heartache and aggravation that you could even begin to compare with the heartache and aggravation of Gert Pinkowitz.

Look to the child, Jerome. This is what your father says to you, look to the child. Because if you want to see what is killing a mother or a father, don't look for a truck, don't look for a bus—unless you know it's the child which is behind the wheel and driving it.

But listen, would you ever hear one word of bitterness from the woman's own lips?

A *saint*, Jerome—the woman is a living saint! Believe me, kiddo, every last word I your father had to pry out of her mouth because wild horses couldn't get this woman to talk and tell you what's what with her high and mighty Tommy.

You know what, darling? In my personal opinion, the entire human race should get together and take off their hat to this wonderful creature.

And I'll tell you something else, boychik. Thank God this is a person made of iron. Of *iron*! Because with flesh and blood you couldn't live with what this woman's got to live with. I as your father look at this creature and I say to myself, "Sol, even with the agony you are suffering at your own child's hands, this is nothing when you stop to compare it to the agony of a person like Gert Pinkowitz!"

This is what your father says to himself, Jerome. Every time I even *look* at the woman, this is what your father in his own mind has to say to himself.

On the other hand, who could overlook the similarities? I mean, when I look at what this woman has her hands full with, you think I don't say to myself, "Sol, when you consider your own trials and tribulations, you don't notice the terrific similarities?"

Jerome, believe me, darling, whoever said it's a small world, the same person could go ahead and say it a thousand times and he still wouldn't be saying it enough.

Number one, Gert tells me her Tommy is a brilliant boy. So even if I am in no position to pass judgment, let's give the woman credit. Like my own Jerrychik, Gert's Thomas is another genius, this much I am willing to acknowledge, even if the Robbins woman, who has her own Harold, says to your father she's read the Pinkowitz boy's books and every word in all three of them she could take it or leave it.

Okay, so it's a free country, the Robbins woman is entitled to her own personal opinion, maybe the woman knows whereof she speaks. But meanwhile, so long as Gert Pinkowitz tells me the child is a genius, then the child is a genius—even if Dora Robbins wants to look your father in the face and maintain to the contrary.

But, Jerome, I ask you, when did the boy last do a little business? Because the answer is don't ask. Not for seasons and seasons. So listen, maybe in your lifetime you ran across another individual where this particular situation is also the case?

Meanwhile, what's the next thing?

No *pictures*, darling! Just like with somebody else your father happens to be acquainted with, no pictures, not even a snapshot in the newspapers—plus no Merv Griffin, no Merv Griffin neither!

But wait a minute, Jerome, wait a minute, the similarities I'm not even finished with yet. Listen. Because is the name which the boy's mother sat down and gave him good enough for this ungrateful child? Like somebody else who is associated with your own father's personal acquaintance, I ask you, is it?

Only *worse* than *you*, Jerome. Worse!

Believe me, worse isn't even the half of it. Because with you, darling, maybe there is a certain degree of rhyme or reason. But with the Pinkowitz kid? With him we're talking a whole different ballgame altogether. With him we're talking it's all the way out of the whole total picture!

Myself, boychik, when I heard it, when the woman is on the premises only an hour already, you could have blown your father over with a feather. The woman does not even have one stick of furniture moved in yet! Do you hear me, Jerome? Not one stick! But meanwhile this is how heartsick she is—the woman is so heartsick she's got to say to the moving man she's sorry but not for another instant could she stand the strain and the aggravation, would he please leave everything sit while she goes and sees who her new neighbor is and gets this off her chest. And do you know *why*, darling? Because if the woman does not talk to somebody in the next two seconds, then she is going to have to scream or take a pill. And meanwhile I don't have to tell you, a pill she can't actually take one way or the other, since so far they didn't unpack the first thing yet, not even the box with her emergencies.

Jerome, I know I don't have to draw you a diagram, to explain to you that it is I your father who is the individual next door.

*This* is how small the world is, Jerome—you turn around and the next thing you know you are the person next door!

Sweetie guy, you could go ahead and send hoodlums. They could bring brass knuckles down here to get me with, but your father wants you to know one thing. In this world, Jerrychik, even if you couldn't believe it, there are worse things than what you did to your name when you made it

J.D., which, by the way, even President Eisenhower himself didn't think was such a hot idea—but, all right, go ahead and look up the history on it for yourself.

I promise you, boychik, you go listen to Gert Pinkowitz with her Thomas, you'll hear and you'll hear plenty—a child which comes into this world with such a perfect name and then has the gall to turn around and change it the instant they come along and say to the boy, "Pinkowitz?"

All right, so the child wanted to make a good impression. So, darling, your father will tell you what happens when all you can think of in the world is making a good impression. Because if you remember Goldbaum, sweetheart, then you'll know who your father is talking about when I tell you the man's son comes home with a *blonde*.

A *blonde*, Jerome, as your father lives and breathes, the man's son comes home with a *blonde*.

But meanwhile Goldbaum couldn't learn to live with it? And also his wife of forty years couldn't learn to do likewise?

So they make a meal, Jerome. Are you listening to me, darling? Mrs. Goldbaum, God love her, she makes a meal. And right off to begin with she puts soup on the table. And the blonde, Jerome, the blonde who only wants in her heart of hearts to make a good impression, she says, "Oh, God, is this soup wonderful, is this delicious soup, never in my life did I have such a bowl of soup!"

This is what the girl says, Jerome. So are you listening? The blonde says, "This soup, such a wonderful soup—so tell me, everybody, what is it, what is it?"

Darling, Mrs. Goldbaum shouldn't answer the girl?

Believe me, Jerome, Mrs. Goldbaum you never met maybe, but let me tell you that this is a civilized person.

So to make a long story short, she says to the blonde, "Matzoh ball soup, we call it matzoh ball soup."

151

Darling, verbatim, this is how Mrs. Goldbaum answers.

But the blonde, Jerome, are you remembering *her?* This blonde which in her heart of hearts only wants to make on these people a good impression? Because I want you to hear what she says as a consequence of she only has the best of intentions.

You're listening, sweetie boy? Was your father born yesterday because he's taking it for granted you are listening to him? Because this blonde which I am referring to, this is what the girl says to Mrs. Goldbaum, and I am quoting you, sweetheart, every single *word.* She says, "Holy Mother of God, it sure turns out better than when they make it from the matzoh's shoulder."

Good impressions, Jerome—this is the aggravation they give everybody. But Mrs. Pinkowitz's Tommy, all the child can think of is how to make a good impression. And forget just a T. for Thomas. *Worse,* I'm telling you. Worse by a long shot.

Believe me, Jerome, the sin you did to your name the instant your father's back was turned, it's nothing by comparison. Even the woman herself would tell you if you asked her. Because I your father asked her, and she answered me, "Solly, Solly, what your child did to you when he made it J.D., take my word for it, it is a blessing by comparison. A blessing, Solly, a blessing!"

Cutie fellow, it should only fly from your father's lips to God's two ears when I say to you in all honesty, "The nerve of some children!"

Okay, so send bullies to knock me down and steal my last red nickel, but your father, Jerome, is no stranger to what a child can do to the heart of a parent. So my tears shouldn't go out to this woman who's got a Thomas just like I've got a Jerome, only worse if you could actually believe it?

Darling, the woman can't even speak when she says

to me, "Solly, sit down, dearheart, because I want you to get yourself ready for the shock of the century."

Sonny boy, I am telling you they could have come in here and blown your father over with a feather when the woman told me what she told me. To take a beautiful name like Pinkowitz and get cute with it? What kind of a child is it which does a thing like this? So if the boy had to have two syllables, what's so wrong with Pincus? But Pynchon, darling, this is a name which makes no sense from every angle, even if you looked at it with a magnifying glass.

So whoever heard of a name like Pynchon?

Tell me, Jerome, this is a name for a serious person? Believe me, darling, your father is willing to learn. There's an area code somewhere where with a name like that they wouldn't all look at you sideways?

So the child could take Thomas and put a little trim on the top of it and *also* make a good impression!


This is why I say to you, Jerome, you have to give comfort where comfort is due. But I promise you, boychik, in this case it's a pleasure, the woman is a living doll, so svelte it would break your heart. And meanwhile, I promise you, it's no trouble. I hear the creature crying both her eyes out, it's such an effort to run next door? So maybe that's where I was if you called last night and your father wasn't here to pick up.

So you called, darling? Tell me, you really called?

You know what, Jerome? I say you used the brains God gave you and you waited for when they knock the rates down and it wouldn't cost you no arm and a leg just to say hello and Happy High Holy Days to your father.

Tell me, sweetheart, is that the right answer?

Save your breath, I guessed.

Listen, you think a father does not know a son?

Don't worry, boychik, when all is said and done, a father knows a son—even with no pictures and a name he could never warm up to. But Merv, Jerome, Merv you promised me you'll get busy and take care of. Because I'll tell you something, darling. If you will pay attention to me with both ears, your father will let you in on a big secret.

You remember when years and years ago you sat yourself down and you wrote about this woman who's so fat and all day long she sits on her porch and listens to the radio? Darling, I'm going back years now, but, tell me, do you remember? So because this creature was so lonely and also dying and so forth, it was you yourself which said, please God, the people on the radio should all get together and do for her their very utmost, since what's the woman got in the whole wide world except the people which are talking on the radio?

Sweetheart, sonny boy, I don't have to tell you it was you yourself which said this with your own two lips. So don't make a federal case, Jerome—is it such a big difference that your father got a *television*? Are you saying to me it's not the same principle?

Please, darling, for your father, and so please God you wouldn't have to contradict yourself, be a sport and go on Merv Griffin.

But if it is so important to you that it has to be a fat woman which is listening, and if your own father's suffering is not enough for you, then Jerome, do it for Gert, darling, do it for Gert Pinkowitz.

So all right, Gert Pinkowitz is *not* so svelte! So your father told a little fib. So send G-men and put him in a prison.

The creature is *dieting*, Jerome. Did you hear me? Dieting! So between you and me, did Gert actually get anywhere yet? So sue me, the woman's not skinny!

I'm telling you, darling, this woman is so fat it would break your heart just to look at her—and all I got to say is thank God 305 is her area code and you'll never have to notice.

Boychik, are you listening? So you're already the most wonderful son in the whole wide world, no arguments. Your father admits it, there never was a better boy. Now go be an angel on top of it, Jerome—for a woman who is fat and is in agony and is a saint if ever I saw one, tell Merv here you come for Gertrude Pinkowitz.

> Love and kisses
> from your adoring father,
> and also Happy High Holidays!

P.S. Did I tell you about Goldbaum is passing away? The same Goldbaum which went on the slave ship, Jerome, the man who has the son which got married to the *blonde*? So he's on his deathbed, and it's good-bye and good luck, I didn't tell you already?

But all right, Goldbaum's an old man, he's got no complaints, that's it and that's it, let's get it over. So did I tell you, Jerome? Because I want you to hear with your own two ears what happens next when the man says to his son which is sitting with him, "Kiddo, you've been a wonderful kid, from you in my whole life long your father has never had nothing but absolute joyousness, so good-bye and good luck and here is a kiss."

And the boy, Jerome, he says to Goldbaum, "Well, you have been a great pop, Daddy, and we'll miss you a lot." And Goldbaum answers him, he says to his son, "Forget it, when that's it, that's it, it's time to call it quits."

So this is when the man shuts his eyes and lays back

down again to show everybody he's ready to pass away. But then the next thing you know Goldbaum opens up his eyes and he's giving the air these little sniffs.

Are you paying attention, Jerome? The man is sitting up, and with his nose up in the air he's going like this, darling—sniff, sniff. So then he says, "Tell me, sweetheart, is Mama in the kitchen?"

And the boy answers him, he says to Goldbaum, "Mama is in the kitchen, she's making chopped liver in the kitchen."

Do you hear this, Jerome? "Mama is in the kitchen, she's making chopped liver in the kitchen."

So this is when Goldbaum says to him, "Look, darling, you'll be a sweetheart and go into the kitchen and for your father you'll come back here with a little taste, and please God, I only got a couple of seconds, so you'll hurry."

Jerome, did you hear each and every word of this? What Goldbaum said to his son, you really heard? Because I want you to hear how his son answers the man. Even if you couldn't believe it with your own two ears, your father wants you to hear.

As God is my judge, darling, the man's child says to Goldbaum, he says, "I can't, Daddy, it's for after."

Did you hear this, Jerome? "It's for after." With these very words the child answers the father, "It's for after."

Jerome? Sweetie boy? Are you listening to me?

There *is* no after!

Now God bless you and let this be a lesson to you.

Three

# [Entitled Story]

——When did you first meet Gordon Lish?

—Nineteen thirty-four. In Hewlett, which is a place about twenty miles outside of New York City.

—Was there anything notable about him at the time? Did he strike you as in any wise out of the ordinary?

—No, not anything I can think of. But the circumstances were special. There was a blizzard that day—the eleventh day of February, nineteen thirty-four. I know this seemed meaningful to the fellow, a sort of sign of sorts. For as long as I've known the man, he every so often speaks to what seems to him to be the significance of snowstorms in his life. You know, heavy snows showing up on his birthdays and the like.

—He is superstitious.

—Oh, sure—but who isn't?

—You kept in pretty close touch with Lish after that first meeting?

—You bet. I thought he was tremendously good company, a placid chap and enormously sweet-natured. Oh, he was easy to be with, all right. Not much on his mind, but what little was there he'd share with you, no hesitation, not the least of it. Besides, it was never a problem keeping track of him. I mean, he stayed close to home back in those days— few friends, few outings, a dreamer chiefly. Guy could sit for hours just staring. It was pleasant. To tell you the truth, it was a comfort just to sit with him—restful, restorative. You know . . . certain persons give you certain feelings. Well, I liked him—I suppose that explains everything.

—He confided in you?

—Whatever was on his mind, sure. But as I've been trying to say, there wasn't much of it. He was . . . what did I say before—placid? He was like that—very placid, very passive—tranquil. Half-asleep, actually—sort of dozing.

—Happy?

—Oh, no question about it—the happiest.

—But then things changed. So far as you could see, what? What specifically?

—You mean the shift in him—from what he was in the old days to what he got to be as time wore on. Well, no telling. But I'm willing to give you my theory, which is that nothing changed in him exactly.

—You mean, things changed around him? The world went from one thing to another?

—No, no, not that. What I mean is that I don't think what happened to Lish was any different from what happens to anybody. I mean, it's not the world exactly—because the world just doesn't matter that much, if you know what I'm saying. Oh, fuck, I'm getting all mixed up. Look, the thing is, it's got to do with time—just the years and years and years of it—witnessing, too much witnessing.

—Witnessing too much of the world?

—The other way around . . . the world witnessing too much of you.

—That doesn't make any sense.

—Well, as I said, it was just a theory—one man's opinion. Skip it.

—But you've stayed with him—kept your eye on him, at least.

—No doubt about it. And why not? The man still interests me more than anybody else does. The thing is, I've put fifty years into the thing, don't forget.

—You see him every day?

—I'd get pretty scared if I didn't.

—Why so?

—Oh, you know how it is—for each of us, there's always going to be at least one person we just can't bear to be out of touch with.

—But what if Lish took himself out of touch with *you*?

—That's just exactly what I worry about.

—But what if he succeeds? What will happen to you if he does?

—You know, that's the very thing I've been telling the man day in and day out. I say to him, "Gordon, the day you look around and I'm not there to look back, that's the day you're going to wish you were never born."

—And what does he say to that?

—Him? He says, "It snowed the day I was born. There

was a blizzard the day I was born. It was the eleventh of February, nineteen thirty-four. It snowed like that on my thirteenth birthday too. Both times, there were such big snowstorms. Both times, there was so much snow."

## End